Pilgrims of Mortality

Don Cohen

Korzenik Press

Lexington, Massachusetts

Copyright 2015 © by Don Cohen

All rights reserved. No part of this book may be used or reproduced by any means, graphic, electronic, or mechanical, including photocopying, recording or by any information storage retrieval system, without permission in writing from the copyright owner, except in the case of brief quotations embodied in critical articles or reviews.

Some of the stories in this collection were originally published as follows: "Mrs. Mintz's House for Sale" in *The Fiddlehead;* "Before the Revolution" in *The South Carolina Review;* "Ten Dollars" in Jewish Fiction.net.

ISBN: 978-0-692-55715-0

Cover design: Tim Kinnel
Cover photo: Don Cohen

Korzenik Press
32 Patterson Road
Lexington, MA 02421

korzenikpress@rcn.com

for Helen

Contents

The Letter from Aunt Max	7
Feast	27
Ten Dollars	37
Uncle Jack	49
My Grandfather's Tattoo	61
C	65
The Robot	73
Photoshop (Gillian in Paris)	81
Before the Revolution	97
Secret	121
Words without Songs	139
On Hearing that an Old Girlfriend has Dementia	151
Samson	155
Mrs. Mintz's House for Sale	161
From Ignorance to Bliss	171
Fox	177
Last Words	181

The Letter from Aunt Max

No need to apologize, my dear, for asking these questions. I have time on my hands to answer them—or try to, as best I can. It's true, as you say, that I've always been more engaged in the present than the past (thank you for that compliment!) but frankly the loss of much of my eyesight and other delights of old age have made my current life not so very interesting. And so I begin to fall into that cliché of the elderly—if not living in the past at least visiting it more and more often. So your request gives a point and a purpose to what I am doing already.

Please give my best regards to your handsome husband and charming daughter. If your busy life allows you to visit New York for a day or two, I would love to see you all. I can even put you up here to save you a hotel bill if that would not seem too much time with an old lady. Believe me, you would be free to come and go as you pleased—I would not be a fourth wheel on your freedom and enjoyment.

To get back to your request, I sense that the heart and soul of your apologetic tone has to do with embarrassment or a guilty feeling that you know so little about your family before you were old enough to see and understand for yourself and not much more about its whys and wherefores after that time. Now that both your father and mother are gone, yes, it is too late to ask them directly. Many grown children of deceased parents have a similar regret. But let me assure you that in your particular case this is not a lost opportunity that would have provided much information if taken. Probably you did ask this or that at various times in your life—questions that, with a little encouragement, could have led to other questions and even a few answers, but I would guess that there was no encouragement forthcoming and little response of any kind except the message that it was better not to ask. Believe me, that is not your fault.

Yes, your parents were reluctant to talk about the past (or even the present for that matter, except for such things as what's for dinner and plans for weekend activities). You ask what were the secrets they were so determined to keep from you (and not just you, I would add). The answer is, there was little or nothing that most people would feel compelled to hide and no secrets of the kind you possibly imagine—no criminal activities, no alcoholism or other shameful habits, no failures in school or business, certainly no political activity, radical or otherwise. So why would they behave as if it was not safe to say anything about anything—which in fact describes their belief and deepest feeling? That would be hard to explain in a few words.

You also kindly express interest in my earlier life. I hope you don't regret encouraging an old lady to talk about herself as you read on (and on!). Possibly I can tell you a story or two related to my experience that helps you to understand your mother and also perhaps your father. You are a hundred percent correct that she and I are different personalities, despite being sisters. That fact is one small piece of the human puzzle you have asked me about.

I should warn you—as if you didn't know—that I'm not so good at sticking to one subject. As far as any point worth making goes, I frankly think it may be better to approach in a roundabout way rather than directly. Or that may be my excuse for a habit of saying whatever comes into my head.

So here we go.

You remember your grandfather, I know, and I believe you loved him. He was very fond of you. Like not a few people, he was a better grandfather than a father.

He was a charming man. In his later years, his captivating smile and wonderful head of white hair gave him the appearance of Maurice Chevalier. (You are probably too young to remember that French performer. If you're interested, you could rent the video of *Gigi*.) Possibly without knowing who it was he was imitating, you may have seen your grandfather do his impersonation, which he would perform whenever he found the least opportunity, singing a song with a French accent (always "Mimi") and shuffling his feet in a little dance. Sometimes he even had a straw hat to wave in the air.

But charm is not such a fine quality for children to live with day after day and year after year. Not so much because it is like a rich pastry—delicious as a treat but not a diet for every day—as because it shines alike on everyone and maybe even more on strangers—it is not a contribution to family closeness. Also (and here I think I arrive at the point that most affected your mother and your Uncle Daniel, as well as myself), a charming person like your grandfather wanted to surround himself with pleasing and decorative people—which seldom describes children growing up in any household and certainly not the three of us.

Without a question, your grandmother was decorative. A pretty woman who took great care with her clothing and makeup and jewelry. There are pictures of the two of them from the 1950s in the Stork Club in New York and, believe it or not, the Tropicana nightclub in Havana, Cuba: a handsome couple at home in those exotic surroundings, like William Powell and Myrna Loy or similar characters in a movie from the 1930s. Your grandmother thought of herself as the queen of Brooklyn, who for some unknown reason deserved only the best of everything. For one small example, she refused to wear any but the finest silk underwear; according to her, it was a medical necessity of her sensitive skin. How do I know? Not only from her mentioning the fact many times but she enjoyed parading through the house in her lacy and delicate silk bra and panties—something I could have lived without. Who knows what went through Daniel's mind when she did that?

In her last years, when she was ill and living with your parents, she insisted her condition required her to eat loin lamb chops two or three nights a week and melba toast every day—not from a package but sliced thin from a loaf and toasted to her exact specifications. Don't ask me what kind of disease necessitates that particular diet.

The Letter from Aunt Max

About your grandmother I would say she was not deeply interested in her children. I believe she saw us as an impediment to the glamorous life she liked to lead, not that we occupied so many of her waking hours. I should also say she was not equally indifferent to us or indifferent in the same way. Daniel she favored most, especially as he grew into manhood; she always cared for men more than women. She had no sympathy for me and my rebellious nature. I think it's fair to say she truly detested that I called myself Max instead of Maxine. (That was not the only reason I did it, however.) Your mother she criticized without pause or pity. I believe she saw her as a rival for your grandfather's affection, not so much because of his warmth toward her as because of her constant and I would add heart-breaking efforts to win his love and approval. When she began to be pretty around age sixteen or seventeen, it only got worse.

Your mother was an awkward and shy young girl, a skinny thing, as timid as a mouse from an early age. The harder she tried, the more awkward she became. Even at ten years old she would want to bring your grandfather his evening coffee on a tray. (When he and your grandmother didn't go out, he sat in his favorite chair in the living room to read the newspaper after dinner with a cup of black coffee and sometimes a square of halvah.) Because she wanted so much to please him, she literally shook with fear of making a mistake. The result was coffee slopping out of the cup—a small tragedy, in your mother's eyes, and your grandfather didn't look kindly on it either. Once—a bigger tragedy—she tripped over her own feet and the tray went flying, coffee spilling on the carpet and on our father's trousers from one of his beautiful gray suits. She cried half the night and off and on for the next week over that disaster. As a matter of fact, your grandfather found clumsiness very much not to his taste, so her sorrow at losing whatever of his regard she had was not completely without foundation.

I was the oldest child and the black sheep, stubbornly following my own path against my parents' wishes. Daniel was the careless one. Some of the scrapes he fell into without thinking were no more respectable than the wicked ways I deliberately chose, but being a boy made them more excusable, at least in our mother's eyes. Ultimately he was his own worst enemy. In his carelessness and impatience I don't know whether he would have been capable of making a decent living. What he wanted, however, was to make a killing, and he did neither one nor the other despite the opportunities he was given. Whatever the opposite of a self-made man is, that was Daniel. He had people trying to help him and still did poorly.

Your mother was the goody-goody, who never told a lie or talked back to a teacher or disobeyed her parents, for all the good it did her. She was one of those people who felt she was being watched and measured and judged even when no one was looking.

To jump ahead to your father's arrival on the scene, it occurred when your mother was eighteen and he was twenty and a handsome, athletic young man. I had already been out of the house for some time, so this was after a particular event I will tell you about as soon as I get to it.

The Letter from Aunt Max

They met at the beach, where each of them would sometimes go with a group of friends. It's no surprise to me they were drawn to each other. If not a match made in heaven, it was made wherever the needs of one perfectly fit what the other is able to give, and vice versa. (I believe this is often the case and just as often the people involved don't understand why they chose one another until many years later, if ever.) To put the story of your parents' attraction as simply as possible, your mother needed someone to protect and care for her forever and your father needed a frightened and dependent person who would make him feel strong and useful while not challenging him. (Although you can't blame parents for everything, it's not nothing that his father was a bully. Always right about everything, or so he thought. If he had met Albert Einstein, he would have immediately told him what was wrong with his theories. He took great satisfaction in reminding your father of the many faults he constantly found in him.)

I could give you hundreds of examples of how this unspoken agreement worked between your parents, some of which are already known to you. One I think of from when you were too young to be aware is when they bought their first house. To spare your mother the strain of even the most trivial decisions, he sent her back to her parents for two months while he made every household choice, from the carpets to the paint on the walls to every stick of furniture, and even the food in the kitchen cabinets. He clothed her like you would choose clothing for a doll and telephoned to make appointments for her, whether for the doctor or the hairdresser. The things he did to protect her from the demands of being a mother, even beyond the long list of domestic helpers he hired, I won't go into here. If you like, we can have a conversation about that at some later date. To what extent she might have become a genuine adult in different circumstances, with a gradual experience of normal responsibilities, I don't know. She never had opportunities in that direction.

It's my belief that what your father gained, aside from the satisfaction of employing his strength in support of your mother's weakness, was an excuse to avoid much of what the world asks of men, such as military service or involvement in the community or even definite opinions about this or that. Whatever demand might present itself, he could answer that his first and only responsibility was to take care of your mother. He went to work (as you know, for his father!) and came home to care for her, so every day he was a nothing at work and a hero at home. That was his life and their life together.

To sum up what I'm attempting to convey, your father built a bubble for your mother to live in and, as much as possible, climbed in himself as well. Though I have described him as the protector (and maybe also the preserver) of her childish state, in a way they were both children, or such is my opinion, which you should take with as many grains of salt as you like.

And yet here you are with all your strength and good sense. No matter how much we know, there remains a mystery in these things. My cousin Sidney—I don't think you knew him—a nice man, a smart man, but unusually homely and more cross-eyed than you can imagine, as well as bald from an early age—my cousin Sidney fell in love with a woman, Hannah, who was every bit as homely and cross-eyed as he was. Making a little joke from Shakespeare, I called them the "cross-eyed lovers" and had a laugh at their expense. Their one child, their daughter Sarah, was so tall and beautiful she worked as a model for several years. One of those surprises of life that are beyond explanation.

So now I come back to myself to eventually get to a story about your mother that I think you will want to hear, though it's not exactly a happy one. I'm convinced you never heard it from her own mouth. It's even possible she found a way to forget it herself. I never knew, with your mother, whether she was unwilling to talk about the past or actually had erased it from her mind.

The day I turned eighteen, I left home to live in the Village. Today much of Brooklyn is full of young life. In those days, Brooklyn—the Brooklyn neighborhood we lived in—was one hundred percent boring middle class families. The subway to the City traveled to another world and a much better one, in my opinion. I walked out of my family home with a small suitcase. I found a roommate to live with, did a bit of this and that to earn a few dollars, and—hard to believe, I know, looking at me today or even twenty years ago—I became a dancer with a modern dance company that had not too bad a reputation in those days.

Was I a good dancer? Not bad, but not so outstanding that I would have been in the company if I didn't have sex with the director—which I wanted to anyway. He was a handsome man, magnetic, and a male dancer that liked women was unusual. A beautiful body, of course, and I looked pretty good myself. When two desirable bodies find each other, there's not much you can do to stop them. In those days, too, some of us thought of sex as a political statement, a declaration of freedom. Some women, I mean. The men didn't need an excuse to have as much sex as possible.

I wasn't a pretty girl, but if you're under twenty and in good shape, you don't need to be beautiful to attract a lot of attention. Especially if you're on stage in a leotard or even less in dances most of which had some sexual suggestiveness involved. I got quite a few propositions, as we called them then, as well as some proposals. Frankly, I was more interested in the propositions. At that point in my life, I didn't want to be what most men expected from their wives at that time. By the time those expectations changed—which I hope they have—marriage became less likely and eventually never happened. For the most part, I don't mind.

To some propositions I said yes, to others no. I suppose I had in those days what some would call a wild life, but it didn't feel wild to me. It felt like being alive.

One proposition I turned down was from my Uncle Dolph, my mother's older brother, believe it or not. I think you may have met him once or twice before he died. (His full name was Adolph, which was common enough before Hitler destroyed half the world and incidentally made that name impossible to give to any baby boy.) He was a successful photographer who made his living taking portraits of show business personalities as well as socialites and other wealthy people.

The Letter from Aunt Max

He was not notably good looking—only a few inches taller than my five feet nothing, with a round head that could remind you of an egg—but he was tremendously successful with women, even, believe it or not, some of the young stage actresses whose pictures he was taking. What was the secret of his success? Not only did he truly appreciate female beauty, he found it in every woman he met, and he let them know in word and deed how much he admired them. He understood that even the most stunning women were uncertain about their attractiveness and liked to be reassured. (This also made him an excellent photographer of women; looking at his portraits, you would believe he was in love with his subjects—which he was.)

Did his wife Nettie know about these constant affairs? Almost certainly. He was not the kind of man who would rub her nose in the fact but he would not go out of his way to hide it either. Yet they stayed together until his death. Why? Well, divorce wasn't as common in that generation as it became later. But frankly I don't think they would have divorced in any case. The fact is, his passion for women extended even to his wife, who was not so attractive in the eyes of most people. And (pardon my frankness) he seemed to have almost unlimited powers of sexuality, so—to be even more crude—there was enough to satisfy everyone.

Nettie's reaction (if it was a reaction to Dolph's behavior and not simply her own personal desire) was to become ever fancier and more extreme in her dress and makeup. She was a good head taller than her husband, bleach blond hair, bright red lipstick heavily applied; her dresses and hats were tricked out with ribbons and feathers, jewelry, and furs of course, even when it was too warm to wear them. You can have some inkling of the level of her obsession with fashion (as she saw it) by the fact that she was almost arrested for trying to smuggle a bird of paradise feather into the United States that she bought in Canada, where it was not illegal. She sewed it into the lining of her coat, but it was somehow discovered at the border. Dolph had to use all his powers of persuasion to get away without a big fine or worse.

In her grief after her husband died, or maybe because of her hope (never fulfilled) of attracting another man, Nettie became even more extreme in her appearance, piling on beads and bangles, scarves and fur and feathers, looking more and more like a tropical bird as time passed—her small eyes darting here and there adding to that impression. As did her constant and high-pitched chatter. Something of interest came out of her mouth only once in a long while and I think by accident, like those monkeys banging on their typewriters.

Sad to say, as she got older her thickly applied makeup and bodily stiffness made her more closely resemble a dead and stuffed bird than a living one. Fortunately, I don't think she ever realized that fact.

Why am I talking about Nettie? Who knows? My only excuse is, one thing leads to another. I hope you're not completely uninterested in such family stories. Maybe too the behaviors of one person help us understand the behaviors of others. Or maybe not.

So I'll finish with Uncle Dolph's proposition and then finally tell the particular event I'm thinking of about your mother.

The Letter from Aunt Max

He came to see me dance one night. I'm sure he enjoyed watching the other young women in the company too, but I was pleased and flattered that he would bother. After the performance he invited me to have supper at a well-known steakhouse in the Village. Having very little money and the physical exertion of dancing every day, I was always hungry. I still remember the platter for two the waiter brought to the table—thick, steaming slices of steak sprinkled with pepper and salt. I ate more than my share: delicious.

I've told you Dolph was not handsome in any obvious way, but there was something about him. He was debonair. That's not a word you hear any more and I don't know what the current expression would be. Maybe it's not a quality people have now. He was also very graceful for a man who was not a dancer, with his own distinctive mixture of a very relaxed movement of hands and arms and stillness while he paid attention to what you were saying, as if no one else existed in the world at that moment. Again a reason for his success with women.

He talked very pleasantly and humorously about some of the famous people he had photographed and eventually about how he would like to photograph me—free of charge, of course. While I licked up the whipped cream of my sweet dessert—still hungry after all that meat—he described the poses he would put me in— somewhat sensual postures, you won't be surprised to hear. He said the pictures could be useful in my dancing career, which was possibly true, though I think I had already gone as far as I was likely to go as a dancer. Age would not improve what I had to offer. He told me it would be an artistic challenge for him to capture in one still image the youthful fire of my dancing, or words to that effect. Then there was his soft hand resting on mine on the table.

"I want to make love to you tonight," he said. Yet another reason for his sexual success: he said what he wanted very directly. However, sex with my uncle who was older than my father didn't appeal to me.

"No, thank you very much," I told him.

"It's possible I can do things you'll like," he said. Maybe. My answer was still no.

I wasn't shocked or insulted by his proposition. At nineteen years old and having not a few sexual experiences myself, I felt an alluring heat radiating from my body and it didn't surprise me that any man would desire me, even my own uncle.

He was a gentleman, so no meant no. Where another man with designs on a woman (as people used to say) would have called for the check and ended the evening as soon as it was clear he would not succeed, Dolph sat with me for another hour, continuing his entertaining conversation. Then he walked me to the door of my apartment building and kissed me on the forehead, as any loving uncle would.

All right. Enough of that. Don't say I didn't warn you.

Not surprisingly, moving to the Village was the last straw for my parents—the last of many. Becoming a dancer was beyond the last straw. Not only did they not come to see me dance, they cut off all communication with me and forbad Daniel and your

The Letter from Aunt Max

mother from seeing me or even mentioning my existence. Our charming father carried some of the clothes I'd left in Brooklyn to the curb for the garbage men to take away. (Years later I resumed contact with my parents, I'm happy to say, although we never became comfortable together. A week before his dying day, when I was visiting your grandfather in the hospital, he shook his finger at me and said, "You!" in an accusing way but maybe with a small spark of affection too. In any case, his last word to me.)

Daniel dropped by once or twice anyway. Our father's strictest orders were just suggestions for him. For your mother, they were commandments from on high.

Which is why it was so extraordinary to peek out from backstage before our performance one Friday night and see her in the audience, shrinking in her seat as if she wanted to make herself invisible, which I'm sure she did.

Not only was I amazed, I was proud of her beyond what I can express. For your mother, disobeying our parents and traveling to the city to see me dance demanded as much courage as facing the guns of the enemy on a battlefield would require from someone else. Or running into a burning building to rescue a child.

Usually the audience disappears from your mind when the music starts and you step on stage. Not that night, as I danced for an audience of one, my sister, aware of her eyes on me even as I flew through the air into the arms of the beautiful black dancer in our company. I have no idea whether I danced well or badly that night. Probably neither. By which I mean there was no major disaster.

As soon as the performance ended and we took our bow, I jumped off the stage into the audience. This was an unprofessional thing to do—my costume of a band of green cloth around my chest and little satin pants no doubt seemed indecent next to people fully clothed, but all I was thinking was to reach my sister before she escaped, which I have no doubt she would have if I had waited to change first. My embrace was from gratitude and delight but also to keep her from running away. I held tight to her wrist as I brought her backstage—If I said I dragged her I wouldn't be far wrong.

For maybe an hour and a half, first in the theater and then at a kind of café (really a bar) we often went to after the performance, she attracted much of the notice not only of the director of the company (my little adventure with him was long over) but of many of the men who typically find their way to the dancers after a performance. As I've said, she was quite pretty at this time and there was additionally something magnetic in her timid nature. She was like a frightened animal in the forest, eyes wide and shivering with apprehension. I think not a few men are fascinated by young women of that description and possibly not able themselves to say how much of their desire is to protect and how much to take advantage.

In the bar—picture a hot, dark room crowded with dancers, artists, writers, and people who liked to be in their vicinity, a cloud of smoke hanging above our heads (in those days, everyone smoked, even dancers), a piano playing jazz, the loudness of voices that have been drinking—one man after another and sometimes two or three at once vied for her attention. I'm sure no one could hear the few words she managed in response, which probably made her all the more appealing to those particular men.

What was your mother's reaction to this unaccustomed situation? That whole time, she was out of breath from both excitement and terror. Expressions of fear, pleasure, shame, surprise, shyness, guilt, confusion, panic, determination, and even a little mischievousness (to name only some) flew across her face in rapid succession. Her face was like a child's that hasn't yet learned to hide anything.

Your mother led a very sheltered existence until that moment, in part from growing up in the dullest part of Brooklyn but equally from her determination to be an obedient and good girl above all else. Some of her fear was certainly from constant awareness of having disobeyed our parents to see the wicked sister who had been banished even from family conversation. Some was from being there—not only the men pressing around her, but the noise and smoke and music and above all a kind of vibration in the air that expressed the hunger of people looking for some excitement in their lives. At the same time, those frightening things were a suggestion to her of what the world contained, a revelation that life could be more thrilling and interesting than she knew. How do I know? The dawning of that possibility was also visible in her face.

In the middle of everything at one point, she put her hand on my bare arm—I could feel the trembling—and said "Maxine"— only my name, but it was at the same time a question and I would say an expression of wonder from someone who had awakened and opened her eyes for the first time. I felt closer to my sister at that moment than in all the years before and since.

It's my belief to this day that your mother stood at the crossroads of her life that evening. In one direction was the freedom she had glimpsed and the possibility of an independent existence out in the world, in the other the dependence of childhood. And the safety of childhood, of course—not that childhood is always so safe. I did not expect her to stay with me that night and start a new life in the morning. That would have been too much change all at once. But I imagined and hoped her experience that night could be a beginning, like a seed planted, that would inspire a gradual breaking away from our parents and especially from her own fears and constraints. I imagined her new awareness of the smallness of her life until then encouraging her to free herself little by little and live in a larger way.

So when she slipped away, like Cinderella when the clock is striking twelve, I did not think all was lost, necessarily. But in fact the world of freedom frightened her more than it attracted her. After that one brief glimpse, she fled back into childhood where I would say she stayed from that day forward for the rest of her life.

Without knowing for a fact, I'm guessing she confessed all to our parents, because it would be a relief for her to face their open anger and disapproval rather than keep a secret they might guess at any moment. Also she may have sought the displeasure and condemnation she no doubt believed she deserved. I didn't hear from her even by phone for quite some time, in fact until after she met your father and she told me of her engagement. I was at the wedding where neither my father nor my mother spoke to me. I believe your mother found an ember of courage still glowing that made it possible for her to invite me against their wishes.

And that was that. For some people marriage is an escape from childhood. For your mother, it was moving from one childhood to another and more permanent one—a never-never land that was the atmosphere you grew up in. It's been my philosophy (which is too grand a word, but never mind) that people have a right to choose their own path in life. If you ask me did your mother live the life she wanted and was she satisfied with it, I can't answer you. The longer I live, the less confidence I have in saying what's a good life or a bad one. It's hard enough for a person to answer that question about herself. I have only a few regrets about my own life and yet could never have guessed that my early years of adventure would lead to my quiet and conventional existence in later years and that many of my satisfactions would be the very things I disdained in youth (like my years of work at Steiner's and the typical enjoyments of a middle-class city person). I've experienced loneliness, yes, and the other side of the coin of loneliness, which is being able to please myself in matters large and small. I have regrets but no complaints. Every path brings you some things and takes others away.

Even so, I look back on your mother's decisive moment that night with sadness. Do I really wish it had been otherwise? Fortunately, such wishes cannot be granted. If it was, you would not be here to brighten so many lives, including mine and, much more, the lives of your husband and your delightful daughter (who also would not exist!).

Well! I hope you think these too many pages have been worth reading and that I have not entirely failed to respond to your thoughtful and much appreciated letter. Possibly I've told you both more than you wanted to hear and less. I hope not, but it wouldn't surprise me.

Once again, please communicate my warmest affection to your family.

With much love and wishes for your health and happiness,

Your Aunt Max

Feast

The waiters had been told to pretend she wasn't there (only a glass of water with a straw at her place). He didn't eat either, her John: lovely kindness. Later he would, swallowing bread and meat when she couldn't see, but not to fool her: thoughtfulness, another way to show they still shared the same life. The others— John's sister and Arthur, Michael's parents, the Dunns—spooned up the reddish chilled fruit soup. (Strawberry or raspberry? which had Ruth decided finally?) Then salad, poking at the jumbles of small damp leaves, lifting their loaded forks.

She was beyond this universal companionship of hand to mouth. And no longer human, if that was part of the definition? At the same time, wasn't she more physical than ever, reduced to her body? Thirst, pain, fatigue, nausea, her bowels sluggish or explosive: death proved the physical, if you needed proof. But the dying animal and the living one were not the same. So wolves skulked away or were abandoned by the pack. And some people, too: yes, the Eskimos sending their elders off on icebergs and, in Africa, possibly, the dying one left outside the hut. Unclean or the fear of evil spirits, but sensible medically, so as not to contaminate; returned to nature in the most efficient way, wild animals doing the dirty work (in Tibet, bodies left out for birds, hadn't she read somewhere?). Eliminating all that nonsense of caskets and holes in the ground (the excavated dirt at her father's covered with that mat of bright fake grass). Better to go off somewhere, not mix up the living and the dying.

But here she was, in the middle of everything!

It was almost too pat, death and marriage, the end and the beginning. They would go to their hotel to make love; she would go home to get on with her dying. Except, of course, they had lived together for two years; there was the baby being passed from hand to hand like a doll, sucking his pacifier for all he was worth. You couldn't call this a beginning. In her experience, life was always middle; things happened before you knew it and by the time you marked them with a ceremony or even noticed, they were in full swing and headed somewhere else. The baby taking it all in, but he won't remember a thing. Still affected by it. He'll wake up into the long middle of his life already underway— started without him. So: middle. Or end, of course, but that was only once. The other ends—graduation, divorce, someone else's death—were really middles.

Cousin Phyllis came smiling over her shoulder, said, "You look so lovely. Such a lovely dress." More compliments than she got when she deserved them. Lovely dress. How far she's come in the weeks since they bought it. Then she had stood at the mirror in the shop—light sheening off the slateblue satin, shallow scoop neck to hide some of the damage—stood, and wondered if it suited her!

Phyllis smiled, silent sympathy, touched her hand and was gone. A woman she didn't know at the next table—young, slim, long black hair—showed her a stricken face, desperate with sorrow, as if it was her own death she was looking at or her best friend's. But who was she? Caught in the act, she looked away.

After the chicken and steak, John turned the wheelchair to face the dance floor. Michael and Ruthie's friends bounced and waved in a mass, everyone with everyone, those group friendships they had now. The baby swung up and down by Laura, the babysitter: lovely young breasts. Untouched. Well, probably not, certainly not, but still fresh with anticipation, hers and theirs: the boys, the men watching now as she bent to lift him, stealing glances. They can't not look.

Turned toward the room, she thought of that strip of paper from chemistry: a test for something—acid, was it? Litmus paper. Here at the wedding, she was like a litmus test of their capacity for honesty, for reality. She found out the ones who could almost admit what she was now, and the others who asked, "How are you?" as if it was still a question of that, who only talked to her so they could not be ashamed later. The young people who avoided her, more afraid of saying the wrong thing than of death—impossible to imagine this would ever happen to them. Awkwardness and humiliation a worse fate at that age.

And here came Natalie steaming toward her, no way to avoid her, her foul-weather friend, long neck bent, pressing and pressing her arm: "... heroic ... in your condition ... so brave ...." A monster of compassion. A sorrow vulture, feeding, and she was Natalie's feast. Why not say, I know what you are, instead of letting Natalie eat her fill? When would she have the right, if not now? Instead, closing her eyes to plead: leave me alone. In vain, but rescued finally by John's cousin Owen saying, "Sorry to interrupt." Don't be, Owen. Thank you, thank you, she silently said.

Oh! He was ill too. No question. It was like second sight, or she was so familiar with the signs she recognized them instantly, like hearing your own name in a babble of voices, attuned to it. And he knew. Yes. Brave man, looking his soon-to-be future in the face. Thank you again, Owen, thank you even more.

Then there was the unknown young woman again, dancing with one of Michael's brothers or cousins, eyes closed, head tossing, flinging her long black mane: ecstatic now. So that was the answer: she was one of those gluttons for feeling—joy, sorrow, anything. And why not?

Michael bent over her and said, "It means so much to Ruthie that you're here. To me too." Matter-of-fact, not asking for anything. She had been wrong about him: young, yes, but comfortable in his own skin, which makes all the difference. At home in the world. She had warned Ruth: don't be in such a hurry; learn from my mistakes. Of course, her daughter never listened, not once, and why should she? The truth we all know at that age: your life belongs to no one else. She never had any power over her. (When she was in middle school, the argument about makeup—something she actually knew! But Ruth wouldn't budge until friends made fun of the dark circles of mascara; the year of the raccoon, she and John had called it.) Never listened to her and now less than ever. She's happy today, her dying mother a paragraph in her story; it makes her more interesting. All of them, something to tell their friends: bittersweet, or so they think.

The DJ put on the slow number that brought older couples to the floor, all those pairings, natural and odd, the showoffs, the shuffling husbands, the little truces and rediscoveries. The wave of sorrow that washed over her was a shock. It wasn't that they danced before—at other weddings a few times like everyone, nothing really—but this was how loss caught you, coming in under the radar. She'd never missed dancing before, but here she was, inconsolable.

Until John came back—wonderful man, how could she ever not have known that?—to lean over her, his face against her hair. She put her arms around his neck, lifting her head, cheek against his chin. He swayed slightly to the rhythm, swayed her slightly until the end and past the end, those tender seconds when the music stopped but not the dance. Then clapped like everybody else.

Well, she gave him this chance to exercise his gift for devotion, his patience, this extraordinary warmth, attention. Imagine Ronnie in this role, or Tim—impossible! They would be gone—literally, in Ronnie's case, out the door at the first unpleasantness, anything that called for humanity, for admitting someone else's. Tim absent in every way but physically, his famous disappearing act, seen but not heard. Instead she had this large gentleness, like a bear wiser and kinder than people, and more than ever like a bear in his tuxedo, a fine and delicate bear, all his clumsiness gone. He was born for this. As if, all those years ago, they had known, had chosen each other for this (she supposed) fulfillment of his nature and her need. Or her nature too? As if, behind the blundering ignorance of life (her life, anyway), there was a true thread she had followed so that she would have him now.

Half the women here were eating him up with their eyes. Dreamed of consoling him, probably, but really of what he would give them: sympathy they never got from their husbands and never would. Who can blame them? Women would swarm when she was gone. Would he remarry? Yes, probably. Not like some, clinging to the first one who puts herself in their way like a drowning man grabbing a plank of wood. Not helpless to put food on the table or clothes in the washer, not terrified of a night or two alone. Never like that and not that kind of woman. Not soon, she would guess, whatever soon meant. But sex of course rears its lovely head. More than that, he will need to be good to someone. The other morning—her pain kept them awake all night, it made them both crazy—he said, "We could drive into a bridge together." But he wouldn't do that to his sister, his mother, to Ruth, the baby. And when he is dying? Not like this. He'll be himself one minute, dead the next—a heart attack probably, one last kindness.

She wouldn't trade an hour of this life, with all its misery, for years with Ronnie. That much she knew. What had she been looking for then, besides a way out of her parents' house? A man's strength. And mistook selfishness for it. Or selfishness is strength, of a kind. Of course dizzy with sex, too, drunk on it; she would have done anything. Yes, and his success, the things he bought her: really for himself, dressing her, placing her in his settings, furnishing his life with her. But she liked it for a while, being his object. It flattered her; it proved she was desirable, because he insisted on the best, there wasn't an ounce of kindness in him. He was so proud of his honesty, hiding behind the truth. She was thrilled at first by the cruelty, too, the way it made her feel alert, alive. If, then, she had seen someone like John leaning over his poor dying wife's wheelchair, she would have thought, "Sweet man," and put him out of her mind the next second.

No, she wouldn't trade this dying for that life with Ronnie. But death itself, if that was the deal? Life at all costs? Yes, probably yes. If I had my life to live over, making the same mistakes, causing the same damage, I would. I would, would, would ...

When the pain opened her eyes she knew she'd been asleep. But where was she? Did the wedding ...? It must have, yes, because this was the reception and she remembered, possibly, the long aisle, leaning on their arms (not John, he walked Ruth), leaning on Philip and someone else, one foot in front of the other. And the priest wrapping and wrapping his stole around their hands: bound together. So: yes, at least that was over.

The pain never left, but the morphine put it at a distance for a time—like someone else's, or hers and she was someone else. Then rushed back with a vengeance, and here it was again: her raw bones rubbed the chair; the music hurt her, hammering away. That's all. Go now.

But John had abandoned her. There: surrounded, laughing, flinging his arms around as he talked (the time he smashed a shelf-full of glasses making his point in a shop!). What a relief for him, to be free of her! He lifted the baby, face to face, took the pacifier ring in his mouth, the baby's mouth taking it back—their little game. His audience of women cooed like doves. His life without her. He had been hers these long terrible months. Now she was forgotten, annihilated.

But no, he turned his head, saw her distress, came to her: back in harness, shouldering the burden. He must resent, regret, but she couldn't see the tiniest sign of wanting anything but her, to be with her.

He loved her.

Understanding instantly, he said, "Time to go," told the others at the table good-bye, unlocked the wheels of the chair. They rolled past the flashing cameras—death on parade—and the hands and voices looming suddenly: good-bye, good-bye. Then Ruth, kneeling in the white foam of her dress. "You're going?" They stared across the miles. She should say something now. She should say, "Be happy." But the words don't come. In the strength of her joy, Ruth says, "I'll call you tomorrow. Thank you," touches her face. Then rustles up: gone.

At the door, of course Natalie again. Vulture wings spread wide, her killing embrace, talons stroking her nerves, she takes charge outside while John brings the car, saying, "No one but me knows what it cost you to be here."

Looking out at the inn's dark garden where the white flowers burn with their own cool light, she wills John to come. The car crunches up the gravel drive and he takes her from Natalie, saves her again.

She should die tonight and become one of those stories: how she kept herself alive to see her daughter married. The power of human will. The power of love! It wouldn't happen. She would be about the same tomorrow, her heart stupidly beating. The parts of the body were tied together like bells on a string. Nudge one and the others clatter. No tumor of their own, the kidneys "stressed," the liver in rebellion. All in a panic except the heart, pumping blood to the dying outposts, business as usual. The last to know.

Riding home in a black simmer of pain and exhaustion, lights stabbing from the oncoming cars, John's warm low voice going on about the wedding. She couldn't take in the words, wasn't meant to. It was the touch of his voice that mattered, and what he told her was, almost there, almost there.

But it was all too much: the huge, ugly weight of her helplessness as he got her in the house, into "her" room (the bedroom upstairs a million miles away), unzipped, tugged off the dress, pulled on the flannel, breathing hard—she couldn't help him. He rattled down the bars of the bed and got her in. She tried to shrug off the IV. Why not fade away, weaker and weaker? Her body craved nothing, feeding on air, and soon not that. Let it go.

But he snapped the tube in place, started the flow of nourishment. His fatigue made him brisk—get the job done. She almost hated him. Kiss on the forehead. Lips. The bars clicked in place. Lights out. A minute later, his soft snoring from the sofa, still in his shirt and pants, probably. Dead to the world.

Now for a moment her fatigue had almost gone away, pain and morphine canceling each other the way they did sometimes, and the jolt of food in her blood. Back soon, though. But fatigue was not her enemy now. Her last meal would be a feast of exhaustion. Or exhaustion would feast on her. At the end, weakness would swallow her up. Weakness and pain. But they were hiding now, off gathering their infinite strength.

So here she was. The IV bag floated in the dark air like a ghost. She listened to the ticking house, to John breathing. The world asleep and she, for the moment, watching over it, still here, stubborn, alive in the darkness.

Something surprising uncurled inside her and she found herself doing what she hadn't been able to do at the wedding. Now, finally, she blessed them: Ruth and Michael, the baby. Owen. The nameless dark-haired girl. Everyone. Released from somewhere within her, a last hidden spring, blessings flowed.

As if she were suddenly someone, a goddess of generosity, the blessings flowed like water, like wine. For all the good it would do them. Or all the harm. Still, the blessings came, silent, unstoppable: Be happy; love one another; live your lives. From my dying world, I give you my blessing, I bless you, I bless you all.

Ten Dollars

When I was seven or eight and my grandfather was about the age I am now, he told me this story:

I left school in the fourth grade. That was the end of my education, which never bothered me so much, to tell you the truth. I could read. I added numbers in my head quicker than someone else with a pencil and paper. What more did I need? I used to say the reason I was successful in business was I never learned subtraction, so I couldn't have a loss. Later I learned a few things from books, nothing important.

So I was ten years old and got a job as a bakery boy. Six nights a week—of course not Friday—I swept the floor and brought wood for the ovens and carried bags of flour and sugar. There were no laws about children working or not working. My pay? One dollar—a week, not a day—and one loaf of bread every morning. I arrived at Fishman's bakery at eleven PM and left at seven, seven-thirty in the morning, depending on when the last baking went in for me to clean up after. There was flour in the air like smoke; it was hot all year from the ovens. Frankly, I liked it very much. The bakers smacked the dough and shoveled bread in and out of the ovens and joked all night long. They were friendly to me. They even yelled in a friendly manner. Also I felt like a big

Pilgrims of Mortality

shot, out all night working to bring food and money home to my family. In fact one dollar a week and a loaf of bread every day maybe meant the difference between surviving and not.

We were five children, not wealthy. I was the youngest. My three sisters, being girls, couldn't work: that was unheard of. My older brother went to school. The family could afford one son to have an education and it wasn't me. Bernie stayed in school until he went crazy about photography, but that's a different story.

Like a lot of men at the time, my father was a tailor. (He used a needle; in my business I sold millions of needles every year.) He could have been a successful man because he had a specialty and his work was always in demand. Exclusively he made clothing for deformed men—midgets and especially hunchbacks and sometimes a fellow with one arm or a leg missing. That's what he learned in the old country and that's what he did here. He said, "Hunchbacks there will always be," which today isn't true, but at the time it was. He was the best tailor of this type in the city; if he'd worked for himself he could have named his price. He used to tell me there was no one in the world that cared for his appearance more than this kind of customer, and there were some who would pay anything for a suit of clothes that fit the way they liked. But the fact is my father worked for a man named Horowitz who took advantage of him and that's who got the benefit of his special ability.

This Horowitz would wait at the dock when the immigrants came and pick out a tailor. He gave him a meal or two, found a place for him to live, and put him to work in his shop. According to him, he was helping out of the goodness of his heart. "We Jews have to stick together," he said. "If someone gave me a hot meal my first day in America...etc., etc." Meanwhile he had a shop full of tailors who worked for next to nothing and made him rich.

Everything bad I know about Horowitz I heard from my mother. She didn't say much, out of respect for my father, but sometimes she couldn't stop herself. It drove her crazy to see my father work to fill that man's pockets. Two, three times a year he would come with a big smile and a few little cakes: that was his method—a penny worth of kindness while he robs you blind. It was after these social visits my mother said what she thought, how he was a crook and not even an honest crook.

My father stood up for Horowitz:

"The man has to live."

"What about your family? Don't they have to live?"

"We're not living?"

Did he mind working his whole life to make Horowitz a wealthy man? Not as far as he ever said. To tell you the truth, knowing my father, he would have found a way to be poor without Horowitz. If he had named his own price, it would have been too low.

So: now comes the time I'm telling you about. I'm on my bicycle coming home from the bakery, with my loaf of bread under one arm. Usually the one they gave me wasn't the best shape to sell. So what? I liked this ride home in the morning. There were people on the trolleys going to work, the milkman with his horse and cart delivering milk, all sorts of banging and bumping—crates of this and that unloaded from trucks. At that time you saw horses and wagons and also a few trucks and cars. The automobile was new. There were women throwing a bucket of water on the pavement in front of their door. It was a lively time of day. This particular morning it's springtime, the sun is shining: wonderful.

All of a sudden I see it lying in front of me in the street. What? A ten dollar bill. Did I ever see so much money in my life? No. Before I believed my eyes I was off my bike and the ten dollars was in my pocket.

Of course I looked to see who might be missing it. A man that lost ten dollars from a business would get fired if not worse. Ten dollars then was more than the difference between life and death for a family. So there was no question in my mind I had to return it. Maybe I would get a dime for a reward. Any minute now I would see a person crazy with worry. But no. No one. I looked at the ten dollar bill again to see if it was my imagination, which it wasn't. Still nobody. I said to myself, "What if this person has so much money he wouldn't notice ten dollars more or ten dollars less?" I could hardly believe such wealth was possible but here was ten dollars and nobody looking for it; maybe it fell out the window of some uptown penthouse and blew on the wind. Meanwhile I'm in the street with people going to work and a man unloading boxes of cabbages from the back of a wagon looking at me wondering why I'm standing there with a loaf of bread and a bicycle.

Ten Dollars

I make myself count to twenty. Still no one. Should I ask if someone lost ten dollars? No. Honest is one thing, stupid is something else. I get up on my bike and ride home, two more blocks, thinking about the sensation I'm going to make.

Whatever I expected, it didn't happen that way. No, I'm telling a lie. My brother made a sour remark—I don't remember what, but that you could predict. We never got along until years later. I wasn't surprised either that Hattie screamed when she saw the money, because she screamed no matter what happened. Fifty years later she was the same: you walked in the door to pay a visit and she screamed because she was glad to see you. She screamed when she heard that Mr. X died or Mrs. Y remarried. She screamed if coffee was a dollar a pound at Waldbaums. Hattie was the oldest girl. Enough about her. She's also a story all by herself.

What surprised me was my mother. She got one look at the ten dollar bill and that was the first and probably the last time I ever saw my mother frightened. She grabbed me by the shoulders—also something she never did—and asked did I want to ruin my life. That made me as scared as she was. Then she brought me into the kitchen and said she knew I was a good boy who wanted to help his family, but how could I do this? She thought I took it from the bakery. I kept saying I found the money on the street. Gradually she began to believe me. Finally the decision was made to wait until my father came home. I went to bed thinking I would never sleep and when I woke up it was evening. My father and my mother sat at the table in the kitchen with the ten dollar bill in the middle like the baby waiting for the judgment of Solomon—in this case Solomon was my father and mother both.

Never mind the discussion—Did I take the money, did I not take the money? Where did I find it? How long did I wait? How did I know no one was looking for it? Then I had to show them where I found it. My brother wanted to come but my father said no. So there I was with my mother and father showing them the exact spot on the street where the money was lying. I could still find that location today. They looked and looked. Who knows what they expected to see. Then back to the apartment and more discussion. The final result was if there was no news of a person losing ten dollars, we would keep it. In the meantime it went into my mother's dressing table.

To tell you the truth, I never saw that money again and years passed before I saw another ten dollar bill. What happened to it? One morning the next week seven oranges appeared, one for each of us, like round flames burning on the kitchen table. Days later the apartment still smelled like oranges. The girls got new dresses, all three at the same time, which was unheard of. Maybe there was more food on the table for a while, not just oranges. Probably my mother saved a few dollars for a rainy day.

All this was very unusual but the most unusual was, my father took a day off from work and gave us a ride in an automobile.

Where did he get it? I don't know. How much did it cost? Who knows? Why did he do it? I have no idea about that either. As far as I knew, until that day my father never gave a thought to automobiles in his life. What can I tell you? Saturday he announced I wouldn't work at the bakery that night. He made the arrangements with Fishman's. Sunday *he* didn't go to work—an amazing occurrence, believe me. Then he says, "We're going to the country." The country! It would have made as much sense if he said "We're going to Alaska." He brought us out to the street. There in front of our building was an automobile, which of course I didn't think had anything to do with us, but my father says, "In, children—we're having a drive in the country."

For maybe the first time in the family, there was a moment of silence: that was the degree of our surprise. The first person who spoke was my mother and what she said was, "Isaac, you don't know how to drive."

He said, "What's to know? It's like a sewing machine."

Well, they both have a pedal and a wheel but that doesn't make them the same. Sewing machines don't bang into other sewing machines or run off the road. Also, my father didn't use a sewing machine; he believed till his dying day hand stitching was better. But nothing was going to stop this ride in the country. Usually whatever anybody else wanted was fine with him but the few times in his life he decided something himself an army couldn't change his mind.

So in we get—this is a big black car open to the sky—and off we go: grinding, lurching; nobody saying a word except Hattie who isn't saying a word either but screaming nonstop. I think all her screaming before was practice for this ride in the car. The engine is almost as loud as Hattie. Not quite.

It's no surprise that my father wasn't such a good driver. Changing the gears he forgot steering and even with his full attention on the gears he didn't know what to do with them. It was a wrestling match between him and the car with a mind of its own, and the car was winning. Plus what did he know about how to get to the country?

My mother tried to tell him that maybe he wasn't meant to be a driver but he said, "No, no. I see now what I was doing wrong."

By hook or by crook, we got to the Brooklyn Bridge.

I'd never been in the country in my life. To me Central Park would have been the country but I'd never seen Central Park either. I knew a few trees like sticks and whatever grew in the cracks in the pavement. The sky? A piece of wallpaper between the buildings, sometimes blue sometimes gray, black at night. Sometimes a few stars. Once in a while the moon. Even on the bridge, not yet in the country, I couldn't believe my eyes. So that's the sky, I thought: gigantic! I held the side of the car so I wouldn't fall into that big empty space. Crazy, I know, but that's what I felt at the time.

Meanwhile here we are, seven people in one automobile. My brother is frightened too but here's a chance to show his learning: such-and-such about automobiles—the clutch, the starter—then on to other inventions. Hattie I already told you. Rose is telling Hattie to hush. Whatever Hattie was like, Rose was the opposite. You'd think she drives to the country every day. Unfortunately she died young. Pearl—this is your mother's Aunt Pearl—makes a remark about a car full of crazy Jews. She always said exactly what she thought. More than once my mother told her, "My advice to you? Marry a deaf husband." As it happened, she found a man who enjoyed her sharp tongue, except on a few occasions when he didn't. Again, another story.

It was the Brooklyn Bridge, so I know we landed in Brooklyn. After that, I can't tell you. Some streets there were big houses with grass all around them. It wasn't the country but it wasn't the city and it was all new to me. My father's driving didn't get better and it didn't get worse. There were a few small mishaps, not what you'd call an accident: once a little bump against another car in front of us. A man jumped out and yelled—he was wearing goggles, which some drivers did then. My father shrugged and said "sorry, mister" and that was that; once a small scrape against a tree. My mother told him maybe we should go back but no, on we went.

And then we were in the country: trees like you wouldn't believe; big rocks; fields with rows of some sort of green vegetable; other places, brown earth as far as the eye could see waiting maybe for something to grow; a farm house here and there, chicken coops, cows standing in a pasture and cows sitting in the grass, comfortable like a cat on a cushion. The road of course was a dirt road; you looked back and saw the dust we made.

Then a field of grass, a little hill, with rocks poking up, a fence all around it, and sheep—maybe twenty-five, thirty sheep chewing on the grass or bunched together nudging each other with their heads. How did my father find those sheep? From that day to this, I have no idea. It has to be a chance accident—what would he know about where sheep lived and if he knew he wouldn't have any idea how to get there. He knew wool, but sheep was someone else's business, to say the least. But, chance or not, it was like this was the purpose of our trip and the whole reason for the car, the drive to the country, everything. My father drove the car off the road, bouncing on the bumpy grass, and shut off the engine. Suddenly everything was quiet, even Hattie, only the gentle sound of a few sheep baaing. A bird or two somewhere.

We get out of the car and my father goes to the fence and looks at the sheep and looks at us and looks at the sheep again. Some of them look back, wondering whatever sheep wonder about, others not. There are big ones and little ones, all covered with curly white wool—in some cases, a little gray, to tell you the truth, but mainly white. My father looks at us again and waves his arm at the sheep and says, "So meet my partners in the tailoring business!" With the biggest smile I ever saw on his face before or since: "So meet my partners!"

To tell you the truth, I was looking more at my father than at the sheep. At that moment, he was the more unusual sight to me.

About what happened the rest of that day, I have no memory at all. We found our way home, but how or when we got there I can't tell you. Did we get lost? I don't know, and I can't tell you anything that was said or anything we saw. Did we eat a meal? I don't know that either. As far as my memory goes, our trip to the country ended there, at that field of sheep.

The next day, Monday, the car was gone and my father was back at work, as if none of this happened. But to this day, when I think of my father, I remember that moment in the country. My father in his dark suit and white shirt and tie, of course, and of course a hat too, as dark as the suit, but dusty from the road. He was maybe five foot two inches tall on a good day and a little bent over from his work—I was already as tall as he was and Bernie was taller. My father the tailor who slaved his life away in Horowitz's shop waving over the fence, happy as a clam, introducing his family to a field full of sheep: "So meet my partners!"

Uncle Jack

The phone rang and his mother answered hello and said yes and listened. He could see from the dining room how she looked at his father and leaned her head that way to tell him shut the kitchen door. After that he could still hear her voice between when she was listening, but not what the words said.

Eleven was the next problem of his math homework, multiplication one to seventeen odd. It was easy; the bottom number was thirty-one so put down one times forty-two is forty-two three times two is six three times four is twelve. At the other end of the table, Jonathan flipped the pages of his car magazine.

Then she must have hung up, because it was her voice talking, then his father's, then hers.

The door opened and his mother came into the dining room. She looked at Jonathan first, then him. His father was in back of her in the doorway. He put the ends of his fingers touching her shoulder. She looked at the middle of the table where there wasn't anything and said, "Well, your Uncle Jack died last night."

He didn't know what it meant, her saying, "well." It sounded like when someone tells a story and they say, "well," so you know it's near the end and they mean, This is what happened. The look she had, with her lips like that, was the same as when he made her sick and tired of repeating herself, couldn't he listen the first time? So instead of being sad he waited.

"Uncle Jack?" Jonathan asked.

"It was unexpected," his mother said. Which Uncle Jack always was. When he banged on the door is when you knew he was coming for a visit: just there he was.

She looked at them again. Her eyes were shiny.

"Poor Jack," his father said. "He was one of a kind. He certainly liked you boys."

"The wake is in Chicago on Thursday," his mother said. "I'll be gone a few days."

Which meant they weren't going too. Uncle Jack was their uncle but he was her brother. When she was little, they went to the same school, only with him in a higher grade. Her older brother. Uncle Jack was supposed to walk her home but he went off with his friends instead. "You didn't have it in you to get lost," he said one time. He told them, "Your mother was born on the right road." When Uncle Jack was at their house, they stayed at the table a long time after dinner. He told about people he was always meeting, like the man who balanced himself on one finger in the circus when he was younger, that was his job, and his finger was as thick around as your arm. After a while, his mother said, "Those dishes won't do themselves." "They damn well should!" Uncle Jack shouted. "I don't suppose you'd help," she said. "I wouldn't deny you the pleasure, Maggie," he said. No one else called her Maggie. That was her name when she was a girl.

In the morning, there was a blue suitcase in the kitchen. His mother wore a dress with her apron on top when she put scrambled eggs on his plate. She said, "I want you to finish your homework before dinner while I'm gone." Which she knew he always did except when he had to do something else. When it was time for him to wait for the bus, she pressed her lips on his forehead for a second. After school, the suitcase was gone and she was too. His father worked at home that day, writing little black ink notes on the pages of his reports and turning them upside down to make another pile, the ones that were finished.

The next day was Thursday. The funeral was at ten o'clock in Chicago. That meant it was eleven o'clock here. The hours happened here first and one hour later they had that same time in Chicago. He pictured a church like St. Brigid's with stairs going up to three big doors. In front of the altar would be a coffin and inside the coffin was Uncle Jack. After the mass, they would carry the coffin down the aisle and down the steps and put it in a black hearse and drive to a cemetery. They would take it out of the hearse and put it in a hole and fill the hole with dirt from the pile they made when they dug the hole.

Uncle Jack was dead.

Every time when he visited, Uncle Jack had a different car or, sometimes, if you got to the door fast enough, you saw a yellow taxicab before it drove over the top of the hill. Uncle Jack rubbed his hair hard and squeezed Jonathan's shoulder and held his father's handshake with two hands. He wrapped his arms around his mother and said, "Maggie!" "You could have called for once," she said. "And spoil the surprise?" he said, laughing his loud laugh.

His pockets were full of candy. When his mother went back to the kitchen, he reached his both hands in and pulled them out full of licorice pieces, chocolates, Double Bubble, jawbreakers, redhots, caramels.

"Come on, boys," he said. He held his hands out until you took not just one or two. His mother's voice said, "You'll ruin their appetites, Jack."

"Sees through walls," Uncle Jack told them.

"I know your ways," she said, trying to sound mad but it was different from when she really was.

Uncle Jack threw a handful of candy in his own wide-open mouth, licorice and redhots and jawbreakers all together.

Uncle Jack came to visit from different places: Cleveland, Buffalo, St. Louis, Philadelphia, Cincinnati, once California, and sometimes Chicago. He told them about when the Ohio River caught on fire. He told about when it was so cold near Buffalo the cows froze into statues standing up in the fields. They broke in pieces if you hit them with a hammer.

"Jack!" his mother said.

"It's God's own truth," said Uncle Jack.

"Leave God out of it," she said.

"You need to get out more, Maggie. Strange things happen in this world."

"Did you hit one with a hammer?" he asked Uncle Jack.

"Saw another man do it. Sounded like a brick going through a plate glass window."

Later he knew it was only a story, one of Uncle Jack's stories, his mother called them.

"If you could have one thing in the whole world, what would it be?" Uncle Jack asked them.

"A rocket ship," he said.

Jonathan said, "Ten million dollars."

"I'll tell you what I'd want," Uncle Jack said. He looked at him and Jonathan and then he said, "Tomorrow's newspaper." He poked the table with his finger and said it again: "Tomorrow's newspaper. That would be worth more than your paltry ten million."

Uncle Jack took them outside and showed them a curve ball. Jonathan caught it. He showed them how to put your fingers on the ball to make it curve when you threw it. They both tried.

When Uncle Jack was there, his father drank beer at dinner and said "she" when he meant their mother. Uncle Jack told about the time he was in the army, in a swamp up to his knees with snakes and leeches in it and one leech got inside his boot and inside his sock. He had to burn it off with a match.

Uncle Jack sang "I had a mule and her name was Sal" or "Down in the valley" when he was getting dressed. His feet thumped down the stairs. He gargled in the bathroom every morning and at night; you could hear the gargling sound from your own room. When he read the newspaper, the pages crackled and he said some words out loud: "Asia" or "senate" or "bailiff." His lips made kissing sounds when he ate. He tapped his knuckles on the walls when he walked around the house. He shouted their names until they came running.

When Uncle Jack left, it was quiet again.

Sometimes he saved a few pieces of candy in his drawer with pencils and coins from foreign countries and baseball cards. He ate one secretly at night, or Saturday morning. You didn't know when Uncle Jack would bang on the door again. It might be a month or a year.

Now Uncle Jack was dead, so that meant never.

When he came home from school he smelled baking cookies before he opened the door. His mother was in the kitchen, washing up the bowls and things from baking. She wiped her hands on a dish towel and brushed his hair smooth with her hand.

"Here you are," she said.

"What was Uncle Jack's funeral like?" he asked.

"It was the way funerals are," she said. "It was all right."

Uncle Jack

She took a cookie off the rack and put it on a plate and poured his milk.

At dinner she said, "It's good to be home." "Here's to Jack," his father said, and they all held their glasses up—milk, milk, water, ice tea—and took a drink from them and waited for a second before they started to eat.

He went outside where his father was making a new brick path. When his mother was away and he stayed working at home his father put little sticks in the ground and tied string connecting them to make a little fence to show where the path would be. That's where he dug up square piece of grass so you could see the path, but so far it was brown dirt. He dumped two piles of sand from his wheelbarrow and raked it smooth. Today he took bricks from the pile of bricks and put them in the sand. After he got a brick straight, he tapped it with the handle of his trowel that was a pointy triangle at the other end to tap it down into the sand.

"You know about Uncle Jack dying?" he asked.

His father tapped a brick and rubbed his hands together. He looked at him.

"How come he died?"

"People die, sad to say."

"I mean, what from?"

His father got a new brick from the pile and put it in the sand, straightening it with his fingers.

55

"You liked your Uncle Jack," he said, "and he liked you."

"Does Jonathan know?" he asked.

"Ah," his father said. He tapped the brick and got another one and put it in the sand and straightened it and tapped it.

"Does he?"

"Jonathan is older."

"He's my uncle too."

"You should remember Uncle Jack in your own way," his father said. But he still waited. "Your mother and I decided it would be best not to talk about it."

"Jonathan knows," he said.

His father took another brick from the pile and crouched down, making the path again.

"End of discussion, Sport," his father said.

Everybody knew except him. He found Jonathan outside doing nothing.

"Do you know what Uncle Jack died from?"

Jonathan didn't answer or look at him.

"Do you?"

"Yeah. Mom told me."

"What?"

"You're too young," Jonathan said.

"Tell me."

"He's dead, isn't he? Who cares how he died."

"Tell me."

"Tell me, tell me," Jonathan mocked.

"Tell me."

"No."

"Tell me."

Jonathan stared at the Frosts' house. When he looked back, he came closer and his face seemed like he wanted to smash him.

"You want to know?"

"*You* know."

"He killed himself. Satisfied?"

"Liar!"

"If I'm a liar, why did you ask me?"

"Shut up!"

Jonathan still looked like he might smash him, but his eyes were wet. He wiped across them with his fist.

"He never would do that," he told Jonathan.

"He shot himself in a hotel in Chicago. He didn't die for two days. He cursed the priest that came to give him last rites. Then he died. OK?"

Before he could say anything, Jonathan walked fast down the driveway to the street. He flung out one arm like pushing away an invisible person who was trying to stop him and ran a few steps. Then he kept walking down the street. Further away he ran again up over the hill until he couldn't see him any more.

Jonathan was telling the truth but he wanted his mother to say he was lying. She was in the kitchen sitting at the table. He looked down at the floor. The dark lines in the wood were called grain.

"Did Uncle Jack shoot himself?" he asked.

A long time ago, when they moved to this house, his father used his tools to pull up an old yellow kitchen floor. The wooden boards were underneath. Now they were the floor. He looked at her. She didn't say anything but she didn't look too mad. That meant it was true.

"Why did he curse the priest?" he asked.

She sighed. It made her tired that Jonathan told him.

"Uncle Jack was his own worst enemy," she said.

"If he did that ..." He didn't want to say what he was thinking but she knew.

"Uncle Jack is God's problem now," his mother said.

At church, he looked up at Father Bailey's brown eyes big behind his glasses when he walked past their pew, talking into his microphone. What would Father Bailey do if you cursed him when he came to hear your last confession and administer the last rites before you died? He knew the way Father Bailey's face could go from serious to smiling to angry to smiling again in one second. You didn't see it change. Usually you didn't know what it would be next. He loved you with Christian love, which meant he didn't either like you or not like you but he loved you. He didn't love if you forgot your catechism, but he still loved *you*. If you were dying and you cursed Father Bailey who was trying to give you last rites, would he be angry or only sad because you turned away from God's forgiveness and gave up your hope of heaven forever?

How could anyone do that and especially Uncle Jack?

All through the day he thought about Uncle Jack shooting himself and cursing the priest. When Jonathan talked to him once he didn't hear the words because he was thinking about that and Jonathan said, "Hello? Anybody home?"

Uncle Jack shot himself and cursed the priest and died. His Uncle Jack. The truth of what Uncle Jack did was in his head as he lay in bed, not sleeping yet. It was another surprise from Uncle Jack, who was always doing surprising things, and even after he died.

Nobody wanted him to know what happened, but now he did. He didn't understand what it meant; he couldn't think of why anyone do that and be punished for all eternity. But Uncle Jack did and he must have had his reasons. So maybe the things people told him that he always believed weren't really true— something else was that would explain why Uncle Jack killed himself and why he cursed the priest.

The mystery of it was like something else Uncle Jack had given him, the last thing, another present he wasn't supposed to have, like the candy Uncle Jack pulled out of his pockets for him to eat even first thing in the morning or right before dinner. He didn't know what it meant but it belonged to him, now and forever. No one could take it away.

My Grandfather's Tattoo

It was on the upper part of his left arm: a crescent moon about two inches high, its blue curved lines faded and blurred by time. It had to have been more than forty years old when he first showed it to me. I'm writing this a century or more after he had it done.

That was long before tattoos became popular among young men and women mildly rebelling against their middle class parents. At the time—it must have been around 1910—sailors and criminals got tattoos, not twenty-year-old Jewish men beginning to have a little success in the world—in my grandfather's case, by selling dry goods and notions. Tattoo parlors were located in the seedier parts of port cities then; he probably got his in the Bowery, not far from where he lived.

I suppose it's not surprising that the needle was dirty. Family lore describes his dangerous illness: the swollen arm, the week of fever and delirium; cold compresses and sponge baths; his angry and anxious parents waiting for the drama to play itself out, hoping he would live to profit from the lesson. This was before the days of antibiotics; the body either fought off infection or succumbed to it.

He was a strong young man. The fever broke and his characteristic smile returned, maybe a little less mischievous than before, maybe not.

As a child, I never thought to ask him why he got the tattoo. I accepted it as one of many interesting and faintly exotic things about him, like his dark, leathery skin and the hint of old-world accent he must have learned from his parents, having been born here. The whole world surprises children and they accept it all; they don't particularly distinguish between the strange and the ordinary.

Now, though, I wonder what led him to that (probably) dim and dirty shop, where he sat with his sleeve rolled up or his shirt off while the tattoo "artist," squinting in the semi-darkness, injected those two blue curves under his skin. Not only was this not something young men making their way into the middle class *did,* there was the Jewish prohibition of defiling the body. He was defying religious as well as social mores.

What I imagine is this: that at twenty years old he saw the path his life was likely to take—the tough, gradual climb from subsistence to sufficiency to plenty, marriage to a nice girl from the neighborhood, probably children—saw that life and wanted it, but resisted the clarity and constraint of those bounded goals, their commonness, the lack of mystery, as if his life were already decided and you could tell its whole story before it happened, as if he were already looking back from the other end. Maybe the tattoo—the act of getting it—represented that resistance. Maybe he thought of it as the first step in a larger refusal, but his courage failed him and it became the only one or the only one that lasted. Maybe his illness doused the fire of rebellion. Maybe he thought it was a warning he should heed.

But of course I can't *know*. Born into an already-comfortable family, I've tended to see material success as *mere* success, hardly a worthy goal, while it means something different and much more to those who don't have enough, and striving for it is a sufficient adventure for most. As far as I could tell when he was alive, my grandfather was content with his life and proud of his accomplishments. He and my grandmother were inseparable, though I never saw clear signs of affection between them. He was funny and friendly. He liked a glass of scotch in the evening. Whatever regrets he had were not visible, at least to me.

Trying to understand the meaning of my grandfather's tattoo, I think back to how he showed it to me, looking for clues, but I don't know what, if anything, that moment tells me.

We're sitting on a bench in Washington Square not far from my grandparents' apartment on Ninth Street. We've just come from a bookstore, where he bought me a Hardy Boys book. He removes the silver cufflink from the white shirt he always wore and places it carefully on the bench. He neatly turns back the cuff, folding it over and over until his arm is bare almost to the shoulder.

"Look at that," he says, turning his body slightly so I can see the faded blue crescent embedded in his dark skin. "I got that when I was twenty years old. Almost killed me."

C

She disappeared from my life before I was seven years old.

I remember a large woman with a kind face—not smiling, but pleasant and calm. I remember her dark dress covering what adults in those days called an ample bosom. Her voice was gentle and slow, as if she thought first about everything she said.

Which made her singing all the more frightening to me. After lunch, she sat at the piano and lifted the lid. While her fingers pranced over the keys—no one else played our piano until I took lessons years later, though my mother occasionally ran through "Heart and Soul," the one piece she knew—while what I later learned were chords and arpeggios rang out under my grandmother's fingers, a huge voice poured out of her wide-open mouth, high and painfully loud in my young ears. It was as if some entirely different person had taken over her body. "Let's Take an Old-Fashioned Walk" was a favorite; it sounded like you'd better go or there would be trouble. She had an operatic voice, people said. They said she belonged to a choir that sang with a professional symphony.

My parents stood nearby while she sang. When the song ended and she got up from the piano bench, I recognized my grandmother again.

Throughout the performance, my grandfather sat in the chair that was his when they visited and smoked his cigar. He sometimes gave me the paper ring that he slipped off before he lit it. I wore the ring on my finger. Once in a while, he would blow smoke into a jar for me. I clapped the lid on as quickly as I could and watched the bluish smoke swirl inside until it disappeared, leaving a greasy film on the inside of the glass.

They were my father's parents. The table was always set for lunch before my father picked them up at the train station; my grandfather sat in my father's seat when we ate. Usually they came every other Sunday, taking turns with my other grandparents. Some Sundays we had to ourselves, especially in the summer, when we drove into the country to buy corn or had clams and lobster at a restaurant on the shore. A few times, all the grandparents came the same day. When that happened, my two grandfathers played gin together. Grandpa Frank smiled and joked and always lost to Grandpa B, my father's father.

I didn't particularly think about the change while it was happening. At first, they came to our house less often and we had a few more Sundays to ourselves. Our visits to their apartment in the city stopped, but they had always been rare. And memorable, because we went up in the elevator, which at that time was still operated by an elevator man who turned a handle on a big wheel to make it go and stop—one direction for up, the other for down— and into their apartment, with its fascinating contents.

There were colorful pictures from Japan on the walls: a painting of mountains half hidden by mist; a wrinkled, bent-over old man carrying a bundle of sticks; people in elaborate clothing seated on straw-colored mats in what looked like a paper house, and a picture of naked woman stepping into a wooden bathtub that captured my guilty attention. There was a sculpture of a fierce red and gold dragon that had been turned into a lamp. There was a shiny black box on a table. When you raised the little gold clasp and opened it, you found a dark green roll of dry seaweed that gave off an unpleasant smell.

And there was my grandmother's piano, with stacks of sheet music on it and, nearby, a bookshelf of thick volumes of more music.

One Sunday, my grandfather visited by himself. A few weeks later, it happened again. As always, there was lunch after my father picked him up at the train station. Then my grandfather sat in his chair and smoked his cigar. I put the cigar ring on my finger; he didn't offer to blow smoke in a jar for me and I didn't ask. Later in the afternoon he fell asleep in his chair and we had to whisper until he woke up. So it was the same as always, except that my grandmother wasn't there. No one played the piano or sang.

Someone told me my grandmother wasn't feeling well. After that, no one said anything, at least to me, about why she wasn't there or why we saw my grandfather less and less often. It became what happened. I don't think children particularly question such changes. At least I didn't. Unexplained things happen all the time; people come and go. That was just the way the world seemed to work.

I never saw her again. I didn't forget her entirely, but her existence thinned out for me. She became a memory. Or two memories, I should say: a vague one of her usually gentle presence; a vivid one of those painful bursts of song.

She disappeared even from family conversation until the night my father opened the door to my bedroom after I had put the light out. Standing in the doorway, silhouetted by the hall light so I only saw him as a black shape, he said, "Your grandmother died."

I didn't say anything.

"You can cry if you want to," he said. Then he closed the door and went away.

Years later, over lunch with my mother's cousin, I learned more. Maxine was the political and artistic one who lived alone in the city, the outspoken one who laughed at my family's fearful reticence.

My grandmother had had cancer, of course. She had been bedridden at home for a year and then (in those days before hospice) in the hospital for the last months of her life, often in pain, growing weaker and weaker until the day my father announced her death in the doorway of my bedroom.

In those days, cancer was almost always a death sentence and was barely whispered about, even when referred to as "C" or "Big C," as if its deadliness made it somehow indecent. Or maybe because of some superstitious dread, like the idea that mentioning the devil invites him in. It is also true that keeping a

C

fatal diagnosis from patients was common practice then (though most of them must have realized sooner or later that they were dying and possibly conspired in the fiction that they would recover to protect those who were supposedly protecting them from the truth; or maybe in this case too because talking about death was thought to be in bad taste).

None of that excuses or fully explains my grandfather's refusal to let my grandmother's brother see her during that last year-and-a-half of her life (as Maxine told me), refusing because, he said, his visit would reveal the secret. He couldn't be trusted not to break down or blurt out the truth. And even if he didn't, his coming all the way from California after so many years away would have had the same effect.

The fact is that my grandfather was a bully. I suspect he got positive pleasure from instructing the doorman of his building to refuse her brother entry and call the police if he persisted when he got word that he was flying from LA to see his sister. And I suspect he got satisfaction, if not actual pleasure, from controlling the last months of my grandmother's life so tightly. ("He was the prison guard and she was the prisoner," Maxine said.) I had seen him in restaurants scolding waiters and threatening the managers he insisted on seeing because of some small or imaginary lapse. And I had gradually come to understand how he frightened and dominated my father in the family business, my father powerless to oppose even the poor decisions and the abuse of customers that eventually drove it into the ground.

As his grandson, I never felt the full force of his cruelty, but there was the agonizing tickling he refused to stop when I was young and, much later, the letter to my college address that informed me how I would disgrace the family if I made good my "threat" to become a journalist. I have no idea where his contempt for that profession came from but, since I was already uncertain about my abilities in that direction, his venomous scolding had the effect he desired. I never filled out the application to journalism school.

I think my grandfather's negative example contributed to some extent to my own mildness and my tendency to yield to what I think or imagine other people want. I know my considerate passivity drives some people crazy. But I suppose that's another story.

My parents thought I was too young to go to my grandmother's funeral and didn't talk about it later, at least in my hearing. Maxine described a line of cars "stretching as far as the eye can see and then some." My grandmother had had many acquaintances and admirers in the musical world. She had also apparently been involved in worthy causes of various kinds ("her one rebellion against her husband," Maxine said) and representatives of those organizations attended too, along with family and friends. Once she was dead, the gates of secrecy and what you might call protective custody opened and people who knew her in life flooded in. I assume her brother was part of the funeral procession, though nowhere near my grandfather.

He was not welcome at my grandfather's apartment where the family sat shiva for the traditional thirty days. Or his understandable anger at my grandfather kept him away and he mourned elsewhere—maybe back home in Los Angeles.

My parents brought me along one evening not long after the funeral. Possibly they couldn't find a babysitter that night.

There were chairs set against the walls. Some of the people in them—men in suits, women in dark dresses—were distant relatives I vaguely recognized; others were strangers. My grandfather sat in a chair near the hallway to the bedroom, with another chair near him that people sat in briefly one after the other, saying a few words to him. Watching that process made me think of a king in a story whose subjects fearfully approached him, said what they had to say, and backed away, relieved that that was over and no harm done, the danger past.

Unnoticed and unoccupied, I wandered around the room. The Japanese pictures that had fascinated me were on the floor under where they usually hung, facing the wall. All you could see was blank brown backing and the twisted silver wire used to hang them on their little hooks. There were rectangles of slightly darker green paint on the walls, showing where they really belonged. A thin black cloth was draped over the mirror near the door to the hallway. When I looked at it, I could still see myself through the cloth, as if my reflection was trapped behind it.

It was quiet: just the sound of whispered voices and occasionally a muffled car horn rising from the street below.

My grandmother's piano was still there and still had sheet music propped up on the music rack, as if someone might sing her songs, but the lid was closed, hiding the keyboard.

My parents sat with my Aunt Elsie, leaning toward her, whispering like everyone else. All the whispering together was like the sound a radio sometimes makes when nothing is playing—the noise of that silence.

I opened the cover of the piano and looked at the familiar, intriguing span of the keyboard: the long stretch of white and the clusters of black twos and threes. Not thinking about it one way or the other, I gently pressed a white key. A clear note sang out in the quiet room. The whispering voices stopped.

Someone—an old woman, part of the family, though I didn't really know her—took hold of my wrist and pulled my hand away from the keyboard.

"Mustn't," she said, and closed the lid.

The Robot

In bed at night, whenever he thought the word "robot," the robot came closer. That was how it worked. To begin with it was up on Lakeville Road. Every time the word "robot" sounded in his mind, it moved. If he didn't think the word, it couldn't.

He tried to make an empty, quiet place in his head, but "robot" came out of the emptiness and the robot moved toward his house. Sometimes he filled his mind with other sounds, like the shouting and a bat hitting a ball and the organ playing at a baseball game. But then the shouting that he imagined saying "hot dogs! peanuts!" starting saying "robot" instead.

After the robot turned onto his street, he wanted even more not to think it, but his mind would go "robot! robot! robot! robot!" and it kept coming and coming.

If it got into the house and came down the hall and into his room, it would kill him.

In the morning, when he woke up and it was light, the robot was gone.

Usually he was awake first and he read something or flew one of the airplanes next to his bed for a while, swooping it over the hills of the covers. Then there were the sounds of his father's shower and dishes in the kitchen. He smelled their coffee getting ready. He usually didn't wait for her to call him. He got up and put his slippers on and went in for breakfast.

· · ·

At night after dinner, she was with him in the bathroom when he was brushing his teeth. When he finished spitting out the toothpaste, he said a poem he heard at school:

Inka-dink a bottle of ink,
The cork fell out and you stink.

She ran out of the bathroom. He waited there for what would happen next. A minute later, his father came in. "What did you say to your mother?" he asked. He didn't answer. His father held the back of his neck while he put soap in his mouth.

· · ·

After his father left for work, she said, "I need you to stay home from school."

He wasn't sick.

She said, "After I put on my face, we'll go out."

That was her makeup. She called it "putting on her face." She had a brush for brushing on the brown powder. Then she dipped her finger into a little pot with shiny red cream in it and rubbed the redness into her cheeks. There was a box of little square colors called "eye shadow" that she brushed on her closed eyes. Her eyelash curler had circles to put two fingers in and a little

The Robot

round cage at the top. She put the cage around her eyelash and squeezed her fingers together, first one eyelash and then the other. When she put on her lipstick, she turned the bottom part of a gold tube and red lipstick poked out; putting it on, she looked in a little round mirror and then kissed her lips together to make it go the right place and then kissed a tissue to make some of the lipstick go on that.

Then her face was all put on and they got in the car.

He sat in front with her. They drove to a place where lots of people were on the sidewalks walking past different kinds of stores and people crossed in front of the car when they stopped at the red lights. They parked at a building that had names on little signs next to the glass door. They walked up some stairs and through another door into a room with chairs against two walls and tables with magazines.

After a while she went through another door and he still sat there by himself.

One of the magazines had pictures of arms and legs and faces that had something wrong with their skin: sores and black spots and white crinkled lines. When he finished looking at that, he looked at a magazine with pictures of people playing golf and then a magazine that showed cakes and cookies and other food and women wearing different dresses and bathing suits. A while after that, she came out of the same door she went in and they went down the stairs and into the car and drove again.

"This is our secret," she said.

"How was school?" his father said that night.

"I don't know," he told him. His father laughed a little.

· · ·

One day Nancy from up the street came to stay with him after school because they had to go somewhere. For a while they played war and slapjack. Then Nancy read her magazine and he played airplanes in his room.

When he heard their car coming back, he went to the door just before it opened. His father had his arm around her at her waist like he was almost holding her up and he was because her foot tripped on the little step into the house. What else he saw was her face was white. It was even whiter up on either side near her hair like there was white powder there.

"Close the door," his father said. He did, and they went into their bedroom.

A little while later, his father came out and gave Nancy her money and she went home. At dinner time, she still wasn't out of their bedroom. His father gave him cereal with a banana sliced on top and too much milk.

The next day, when he came home from school, she was standing in the middle of the kitchen turning slowly around and around and around.

"Where?" she asked. She was still turning around.

"Where are the ... things for the table ... spoons?" she asked.

The Robot

He showed her where they always kept them.

· · ·

During the day he never thought about the robot. Only at night as soon as he was alone in his room.

"Lights out," his father said, closing the door, and almost right away his mind started saying "robot."

He tried to make it think something else—he tried to make it say "elephant" instead—but it said robot a hundred times and he knew the robot was on his street now and getting close to his house, maybe already in the driveway.

· · ·

When he got home from school one day, she wasn't there. Nancy was. They didn't play cards this time.

After his father came home and gave Nancy her money, he sat him in the living room where they never went except a few times when there was company they didn't know very well.

"Your mother needed to go away for a while," his father said.

He didn't ask where.

"Not for very long," his father said. "Nancy will be here when you come home from school."

He looked out the window. He could see the branches of the tree on their front lawn waving because it was windy today, but sunny too. It wasn't raining.

His father patted him two times on the head and walked away into the TV room.

Later a delivery person brought pizza that had cheese and meat on it. That was their dinner.

• • •

A few days after that, when Nancy was sick, his father drove him somewhere and told him stay in the car, he would be back soon.

His father went into the big building across the street that was made of brick with four rows of windows on the four different floors. Each row was eight windows. That made thirty-two windows. That was where she was but he didn't know which was her window.

• • •

That same night the robot came closer and closer: onto their street and past the Peterson's house. For a little while it was like white smoke filled his whole head; there was no room for words and the robot stopped. Then the smoke started to go away. His mind whispered "robot, robot" in his ear and it moved again.

He tried to imagine the store he liked to go to that had counters with different sections separated by little glass walls. One section had pink rubber balls piled up and a few sections had different kinds of marbles and there was a section with red and silver boxes of cap gun caps, five rolls in each box. But it was like he could hear someone else in the store saying "robot" and it came closer, up the driveway and up the walk to their front door and into their house.

He knew it was in the hall outside his room so he had to stop thinking the word, but he couldn't. His mind went "robot, robot, robot." It wouldn't listen to him telling it to stop because the robot was right outside his door.

All he could do now was hold his breath and not move a muscle. Maybe if he kept still, not even breathing, as if he wasn't really there, maybe then the robot wouldn't kill him this time.

Photoshop (Gillian in Paris)

On the path that runs diagonally through the park, Gillian laughing, arms out, head tilted, as if dancing. Using the masking filter, he traced the gentle incurve of her left side, painting a blue track along the edge of the yellow sundress. He followed the outward flare below her waist, the jog left across the gap between the hem and her leg, then down bare skin. Zooming to 400 %, he traced her sandaled left foot, moved up the inside of her leg, across at the hem, and down again, outlining her right leg. Then up the right side of her dress. The hardest parts were the spread fingers of her outstretched hands and her hair, the loops and twists of those dark curls.

Clicking on her outlined figure with the bucket icon covered Gillian with a green wash. He chose "Preview" and the park disappeared, replaced by the gray and white checkerboard of a transparent background. Working slowly at high magnification (the image breaking into square colored pixels), he used the Cleanup tool to remove traces of grassy background from her hands and hair and the right side of her face. Clicked OK, saved Gillian as a new file: "GSumDrs.psd." It was 9:50. The street was quiet, people long home from work, settled in front of their TVs.

When he opened "NotreDame1.psd" the plaza in front of the cathedral's triple arched doorways appeared within the frame of menus and palettes: tourists in bright colors with backpacks and shopping bags; to the left, an artist in black at his easel, a couple gawking over his shoulder; a ragged cluster of pigeons and, luckily, a clear space in the right foreground. He pasted Gillian as a new layer. He would need to make her slightly smaller and adjust hue and saturation to match the cooler light of the Parisian scene. He might use the burn tool to darken the pavement at her feet a bit. So there was work to do. Still, there she was, Notre Dame over her right shoulder, her joyful little dance now saying, "Here I am, finally in Paris."

When he thought to check the time again, it was just after 12:30 in the morning. Another few minutes, he thought, to blend her figure with the background by blurring the edges slightly. Then he re-adjusted the saturation. Suddenly it was 1:25. He backed up the saved file ("GNotreDame.psd") to the external drive.

In his dreams that night he simultaneously inhabited and manipulated the plaza, but waking up he had no memory of Gillian there, only a sense that his stroking away the birds that hung motionless in the air had something to do with preparing the way for her, conjuring her into the scene.

Homeroom, Algebra 1, second period free. Avoiding the teachers' lounge, he sat on a bench outside near the loading dock and planned tonight's picture: Gillian looking up at the Eiffel Tower. Norm Abrams came out to smoke and sat next to him, immediately launching into another story about the stupidity of his so-called colleagues in the so-called science department. Fortunately, Norm's monologues didn't call for response; as long as you didn't run away, he was satisfied.

In third period geometry, he couldn't remember where they had left off Friday. Paul Hamburg, acknowledging the groans of his classmates with a little bow, reminded him: proof, page number, the problems he'd assigned.

The day dragged itself along.

Ten minutes after the final bell, Melanie Hepworth (short, tightly curled chestnut hair, a sophomore, cute and aware of it) appeared in the doorway of his classroom. Like so many of the girls, she showed a strip of bare flesh between her top and jeans. In his time as a teacher, he had never been indifferent to the sexuality of teenage girls, but the attraction had been mild and hypothetical—and fortunately was still only that.

She held out her elementary algebra textbook in both hands, as if offering it to him, or—more to the point—giving it back.

"I don't understand any of this," she said, with an undercurrent of resentment: why should I try? Every year, a student or two had trouble grasping the idea that x could represent different values; they wanted it to mean one thing and be done with it. "Welcome to the world," he wanted to say. But didn't, of course.

They sat at two student desks facing each other. He wrote "$x + 3 = 7$" on a yellow pad and turned it around for her to see.

"You need to get x alone on one side of the equation to know what it equals," he said. The look of dull panic told him that wasn't the place to start.

"Let's think of it as a question. What plus three equals seven?"

"I don't know," she said, automatically.

"What number, added to three, will give seven as a total?"

"Four."

"That's right. So x equals four."

He took another shot at the idea of isolating x. She nodded. For half an hour, he led her through simple linear equations plus a couple of word problems: if John worked thirty hours and earned $270 .... At moments the clouds parted, a gleam of understanding lit her face, and she solved two or three problems in a row. Then a small new wrinkle—dealing with a fraction of x—made her forget everything; even the simplest equations buffaloed her again.

"You *know* this, Melanie," he said, and her eyes gleamed with tears.

When the class got to quadratic equations, the idea of x having two possible values would throw her completely.

On the way home he stopped at Hannaford's, where he bought a loaf of French bread and a package of pork chops, one for

Photoshop (Gillian in Paris)

dinner, the other to bring to school for lunch. He and Gillian had almost always shopped for the week, but now a quick daily walk through the store with a hand basket had become part of his routine.

At 5:45, he salted and peppered the chops and dropped them in the hot skillet. One of his rules: never eat before six. Tonight, a pork chop, a raw carrot, some of the bread. Ten minutes after he sat down, he put his plate in the dishwasher, washed and dried the skillet, and got back to the computer.

A three-quarters view of Gillian (jeans, rust-colored blouse) in front of their apartment, looking up. (At what? He didn't remember.) This would be tricky, the light stronger and shadows sharper than in the picture of the Eiffel Tower he wanted to put her in. After extracting her figure, he used the Healing Brush to remove the narrow shadow of a small branch on her cheek. As soon as he pasted her into the Eiffel Tower image, he saw that the angles were wrong. Scaling her and moving her closer to the tower didn't help. He tried rotating her around a vertical axis, but that created a weird distortion that was even worse.

Browsing through his folders of Paris pictures, he found one of a park or courtyard with a gravel path and a line of trees, their tops trimmed to leafy cubes. He put her on the path. Yes, he could get this one to work. He'd have to find another Gillian for the Eiffel Tower.

When the clock radio went off the next morning, he woke up sprawled diagonally, his head on Gillian's pillow. He felt a quick thump of grief in his chest, but the pain was like a kind of connection. Gray morning light leaked around the edges of the window shades; the newscaster's voice went on about something. When the feeling began to fade, he got up and showered.

They had talked about Paris on their first date—what they came to think of as a date once they were living together. Going out for coffee after the staff meeting was his idea, one of the few times he had taken the initiative with a woman. He had taught math for three years at Kennedy High and she was new, a French teacher; but even at her first meeting, when she was (he later discovered) uncharacteristically reserved, she glowed with warm energy.

At the Starbucks a few blocks away, she told him she had spent a semester in Montreal but had never been to France: "money," she said simply and, later in that first, long conversation, added that her mother's cancer had been discovered the summer she planned to spend there and she went home to her parents instead, staying until her mother's death that fall (the cancer brutally, mercifully fast) and a month longer with her father.

When he confessed to three days in Paris during his European trip after graduation, she wanted every detail—much more than he had noticed or could remember. The clichés he offered embarrassed him. He had shuffled through Notre Dame with a few thousand other tourists, in the Louvre waited his turn to discover that the Mona Lisa was small, walked down the Champs Elysées, climbed stairs part way up the Eiffel Tower. He most vividly remembered looking for a cheap hotel and cheap food—the café he stumbled on where a sandwich of paté on crusty French bread and a glass of red wine at a sidewalk table gave him a sense of well-being for an hour. She asked about places he had never heard of—Père La Chaise, the Rodin Museum, Rue Mouffetard. Paris was the one place she *had* to see. In the conversation he was already carrying on with her in his head, parallel to the spoken one, he said, "We'll go together."

In the hallway outside the cafeteria, the shrill racket of student talk coming through the doors, Debbie Peterson put her hand on his forearm.

"I worry about you," she said, with that smile—sympathetic but conspiratorial, as if saying, "We both know I mean so much more." Irony was part of her teaching style. Appropriately enough, probably—her subject was history. The students who got it loved her. She and unironic Gillian had not been friends.

"I'm fine," he said, with a pointless burst of laughter.

"*Fine*," she mocked.

"One day at a time," he said, laughing again, angry at himself for falling in with her tone, the weakness it showed, and what felt like disloyalty.

"Michael," she said, touching his arm again. He kept still so as not to respond to the sympathy, the mockery, the invitation.

He watched her walk down the empty hall, the slow sway of her hips in the green skirt, knowing she knew he was watching.

Twice, studying and adjusting his Gillians in Photoshop, following the line of her cheek, the curve of her breast, dodging or burning her blouse or her jeans or skirt to match the light of the picture he placed her image in, he gave in to sexual stirring he felt. He didn't know why that seemed worse, afterwards, than his occasional indulgences in the infinite world of internet pornography. Didn't want to think about it.

Within a month of their first conversation, they had two dinners out, a walk along the Charles, a movie, a concert, half a dozen coffee dates. He couldn't believe she kept agreeing to go out with him and even (the concert, some of the coffees) asked him. But by the end of the month they were a couple; there was no reason to ask because they spent all their time together. They talked openly about going to Paris, and promised themselves they would go within a year, two at most.

He could tick off the reasons it hadn't happened in their more than six years together, five married, but it still seemed a gigantic and incomprehensible mistake. There was the year he taught summer school, the year they moved, the school trip they signed up to chaperone that fell through when a bomb exploded in the Paris metro. Then Gillian's first cancer diagnosis.

Her chemotherapy started in the spring and continued into the beginning of the next school year. They should have gone the summer after that, should have—could have—found a way, but they had no money (the medical costs insurance didn't cover and then new brakes, a new radiator for their Corolla) and they were offered free use of a cabin in the Cantons de l'Est in Quebec—a chance, at least, for Gillian to speak French to shopkeepers and waitresses. They should have gone anyway, borrowed money to pay for the trip, maxed out their credit cards, but they did not know or were not ready to admit that there might not be time later. Or *he* wasn't (reading, later, the thought behind Gillian's faint smile when they decided on Quebec; the growing suspicion that she had been protecting his belief in their future filled him with self-loathing).

All fall and into the winter he worked on the pictures. School followed its usual course, but week by week it seemed more unreal, a recurrent and senseless dream. Whatever got in the way of his Photoshop time was the enemy. The effort to hide his ferocious impatience to get back home was exhausting, but he revived at the computer. He put Gillian outside a grocery on Rue Mouffetard near crates of gleaming produce: peaches, plums, grapes, leeks, green beans, radishes. There she was on the plaza in front of the white extravagance of Sacre Coeur, in front of bookstalls set against a stone wall overlooking the Seine, in a market filled with caged birds. He broke his rule about not having dinner before six, eating as soon as a got home to give himself uninterrupted hours with Gillian in Paris.

His mother called and asked him to come for a few days over Christmas.

"I have a lot to do."

"It's vacation."

"It's a long drive, Mom."

"You're not happy," she said.

"I'm busy."

He told her, yes, he was eating, yes, he was sleeping, yes, he would spend time with friends during vacation—only the last of those an outright lie.

Vacation, finally, and for ten days he lived at the computer, working on pictures of the Luxembourg Garden, which she had especially longed to visit. There was Gillian next to a puppet theater. Gillian looking down at the greenish water of the Medici fountain: he gave the faintest possible green cast to her face and found a way to suggest glints of light reflected off the water (after undoing his mistakes again and again in the history palette). Gillian near a marble balustrade; Gillian against the tall black spikes of the iron fence surrounding the garden.

Wearing shorts and sandals, Gillian stood on the dusty ground in front of a broad, low pool edged in granite, where a boy was nudging a sailboat with a stick. He had to teach himself how to work with a directional light source to blend her into the sunny scene. For three hours (loading a tiny brush with the sand color at her feet, adjusting transparency, unmaking his bad decisions in the history palette), he tried to put a realistic film of dust on the dark straps of her sandals. Succeeded, finally, and she was suddenly *there*, as if she had come down the broad stone stairs

Photoshop (Gillian in Paris)

and walked to this spot and after the picture they would sit and watch the French families enjoy their Sunday afternoon, then find a small restaurant somewhere in the neighborhood. That was the time he worked all night, surprised when sunlight glared off a corner of the monitor.

The web site would be simple: a title, "Gillian in Paris," a brief introduction ("These are pictures of Gillian's first and only trip to Paris, a city she loved."), and the photos. Without the web and the possibility it offered to send the pictures out into the world, he wouldn't be doing this. Kept to himself, they would be a sad, sick joke, but in that vast public space they would have a kind of life, even if only a few people came across them while looking for something else. As far as those casual visitors knew, they would be real photos of a real trip. Somehow that made all the difference.

School started again January 3rd. He woke up before the alarm and sat by the phone, wanting to call in sick but seeing the danger. He showered and dressed, drank his coffee and ate his toast, drove to work. He sat in his car in the teachers' parking lot until Jeff rapped on the window.

Gillian's course of treatment had been typical, he supposed, except that she was young. Most patients in those hospital waiting rooms were elderly or looked it (Gillian always greeting her fellow "chemonauts" as she called them, the same tired faces week after week). Nausea, fatigue, her beautiful dark hair left on her pillow, in the sink. Her students sent stuffed animals, flowers, and homemade get well cards in French with errors that touched her more than perfection would have—the fact that they would try; the sincerity of their broken French. He still glanced through them occasionally: *chere madam Paulson, je suis triste parce que vous avez une maladie; chere madame Paulson, sentez mieux vitement.*

Then those few hopeful months: her strength coming back, her appetite, really making love again (not just for his relief, which had made him grateful and ashamed), the triumphant return to school, half time at first, but still.

The following June, what he pictured as the rising curve of her health flattened and turned, a grim parabola, the bad news only confirmed by the tests.

Their conversations about going to Paris as soon as she felt up to it went on for a few weeks after that, powered by a kind of hopeful inertia (again, he thought, *my* hope) until she said, "Michael, it's not going to happen." They watched films set in Paris almost every night. *Amélie, Angel A, Au bout de souffle, Le ballon rouge, Fauteils d'orchestre, Paris je t'aime, Les quatre cents coups.* She wanted the subtitles turned off, so he only gradually and partially understood what was going on. But the themes were clear: love, rage, pursuit, sorrow, joy, loneliness, greed, jealousy, triumph, death. All played out in the apartments of Paris, the dusty parks, the cafes, the white streets, on the quays and bridges overlooking the dark gleaming river.

She loved Paris because of the language, of course, and the literature where (she told him) the city was more character than setting. Also the abundance there of art, good food, intellect; the drama of its long history of violence and hope. And something that had to do with freedom and possibility. Paris embraced the things the people she had grown up with feared and disapproved: passionate love; pleasure; play. The cafes, the markets, the gardens, the hotel rooms, the scale of the city and its river unapologetically catered to human desire—celebrated it. She once said, laughing at herself but meaning it, Paris didn't believe that mind and body were separate, no matter what Descartes had claimed. Would she have been disappointed in the reality of Paris? Not a chance.

The trickiest picture was of Gillian at a café. He had dozens of photos of her seated: on a bench, in lawn chairs, in cafés and restaurants in Cambridge, Boston, or New York—their brief shared history of food, drink, and talk, those favorite moments. The angles from which the pictures were taken, the chairs with arms that partly blocked her body, table edges, Gillian's posture prevented them from fitting the pictures of Parisian cafes he took from the web. The obvious falseness of his first attempts (the differences in perspective and lighting, the impossibility of getting Gillian to sit convincingly at any of those café tables) would have undermined the whole project, calling attention to the artifice of the other pictures. Then he found a photo of a café with little round tables on the sidewalk and the same round-backed wicker chairs as the Greenwich Village cafe where they drank coffee years ago. It still took him a week to get it right: Gillian in green under the red awning of *Les editeurs* in Saint-Germain-des-

Pres, looking out toward the street—toward him—two white espresso cups on the table in front of her.

At the memorial service at school the gym bleachers had quietly seethed with the girls' sorrow and the boys' sullen gravity. One after the other, her former students stepped over the power cord taped to the polished floorboards on their way to the lectern and told their touching stories: Mrs. Paulson knowing every student's name at the end of the first week, the croissants she brought to class, her smile, her laugh, the way she talked about Paris, Paris, Paris. They claimed she had changed their lives. Some of the girls cried; one sobbed dramatically. They secretly relished this brief contact with "real life," their little invigorating sip from the cup of grief. One girl remembered the way Gillian smoothed her hair back with both hands. Near the end a tall boy leaned down to the microphone and got a laugh saying, "No offense, but Mrs. Paulson was a babe." He sat perfectly still, a weak smile on his lips. He wanted to strangle the bastard.

He preferred people who never mentioned his "tragedy." Best of all were those who avoided him because they didn't know what to say or feared misfortune was contagious. (Bert Wishardt squeezing his bulk between the noses of cars and the wall so he wouldn't have to face him in the parking lot!) Then there was Debbie Peterson, the animal heat of her compassion. He didn't want to be consoled by Debbie. He didn't want anyone to touch him.

By the middle of March he was done. He knew it, but he couldn't stop, not right away—couldn't face the loss.

He tweaked and tweaked the pictures, reworking them almost pixel by pixel. Then one evening, a Tuesday, he only looked, clicking through them over and over. Outside, the rain had stopped but the sound of passing cars told him the streets were still wet. Any more manipulation would only begin to unmake the hours of careful matching and adjustment. He was finished. He told himself it was only Gillian's image he had spent all these evenings with, he hadn't had *her*.

There was still the web site to build. That would be something, but not enough. It would feel less intimate. He would be giving up what almost felt like being with her, touching her.

He moved the mouse down the File menu to highlight "Quit Photoshop" but didn't release the button for a long time. Another car hissed down the street. It was the end of his communion with Gillian—no, with her image, he told himself again; but also with her longing for Paris, her passion. And he would lose the ability to control a world: a two-dimensional world, infinitely thin, yes, but every element of it under his control, available to be moved, shaded, sharpened, resized, made to vanish or reappear. Already he missed that illusion of power (or the reality of power over an illusion). It was only pixels, it was ones and zeroes, microscopic circuits switched on or off, but richer than the empty world his body inhabited now.

He released the mouse button and the image of Gillian at the café disappeared. Gone. Gone the Photoshop menus, toolbars, and palettes. Gone the false, consoling promises made by the program's tools and commands: the Magic Eraser; the Healing Brush; Revert; Replace; Refresh; Restore; Undo; Save.

Before the Revolution

NEW HAVEN, 1970

Paul, Fran and I go to a rally at the hockey rink. There are No Smoking signs but people light up cigarettes and pipes in defiance of the Establishment. A smokecloud hangs over the un-iced rink, where the speakers' platform is.

People talk about the Panthers, the War, New Haven's slums, the responsibilities of the University, the demonstrations planned for Mayday. The best speakers are black. An enormous black woman in a housedress—the head of some local coalition—hoists herself up on a table and speaks, thickening her accent to meet and mock our expectations:

"Folks tell me they call it Mother Yale. Well, your Mama Yale's been wipin' your noses and your *be*-hinds for a long time now, but one a' these days you gonna have ta grow up and leave your ol' Mama. Now, we don't have no mamma takin' care of us but we's still gonna get what we want. We's gonna have what we are being *de*-prived of and it don't make no difference ta us who's tryin' ta help us or hurt us 'cause we's gonna get what's ours in the end."

We're all impressed. Fran chuckles appreciatively. Leaning over the railing to get a closer look, Paul says:

"She's great! Isn't she great? I want to *be* that woman!"

•   •   •

The fact that Paul and I are such different physical types has kept our friendship going—that and sharing the miseries of graduate school. Each of us sees the other as slightly exotic; each is flattered by the other's interest. Paul is blond and slim, taller than I am, with pale blue eyes that don't tell me much. People will still mention his boyish charm when he's forty. He makes me think of Cokes down at the corner store, a basketball hoop over the garage, dates with the blondest cheerleader. (Paul claims he was too shy to ask.) I'm stocky and swarthy, linked in Paul's mind to all that Semitic suffering and intellectual passion, which he has collectively labeled *Kulturschmerz.*

Lately, though, Paul has been the sufferer. He wraps his hands around his coffee mug and mopes, looking like the one who dropped the pass that lost the big game. He and Loretta are having problems. Loretta is a secretary in the English Department office. Blond, with a girlishly pretty face, she looks like the cheerleader he didn't ask out in high school. They've been married for two years.

When Paul sees Fran he perks up. She's dark too. She flirts with him, calling him "the beautiful boy," and her husky sexiness makes him giggle. Fran has a reputation for being unhappy as well as brilliant but I've never seen her when she wasn't enjoying herself. At *Charlie's* she goes from table to table getting signatures on a petition—Free Bobby Seale—and we can hear her deep laugh across the room.

Whenever Paul and I badmouth doctoral theses in general she puts her hands on her hips and leans back away from the conversation. She's serious about hers, which she thinks will be very good: "important."

· · ·

Two fellows talking in the dining hall:

"What I mean is there's no reason I shouldn't take a knife and stab you in the heart."

"You'd go to jail."

"There's no reason I *shouldn't* go to jail. There's no reason I shouldn't be a convicted murderer instead of a doctor. On the other hand there's no reason I *should* take a knife and stab you in the heart. There's no imperative either way, if you see what I mean. It doesn't make any difference what you do."

"That's such bullshit."

· · ·

Professor F. tells us that essays late by reason of political involvement will not be penalized. He begins the seminar on the sincerity of *Lycidas* with an outline of the critical debate and then asks for our responses to the poem. During the silence that follows, he takes off his glasses and rubs the bridge of his nose. He looks tired. He always looks tired. Five years ago he burned the manuscript of a book he had been working on for a decade and a half, a new theory of criticism that didn't pan out, and his fatigue seems a direct result of the act of feeding his typescript to the flames. Paul is full of admiration:

"He's made himself an emblem of failure, a tragic hero."

I'm curious about the immolation scene itself and wonder whether there was more pain or pleasure in it, more loss or more liberation.

Professor F. says:

"If your work here is worth doing at all it's worth doing now, when its value is being questioned and its existence, to some extent, is threatened."

Carla Handman starts the discussion. Her specialty is unearthing fraud and pretension and now she badgers Milton for a while: the poet is more concerned with himself than with the supposed friend who died.

Benson raises a pale hand and defends the poem:

"I think one of the most important things literature can do is find dignified forms for sloppy feelings."

Benson's comments always sound prepared. I picture him alone in his room surrounded by unwashed dishes and piles of books, trying out his phrases on a tape recorder.

•   •   •

Someone did a job on the library steps during the night. The word "Unite" has been painted over and over again on both treads and risers, in black, twenty-eight times in all:

UNITE UNITE UNITE UNITE UNITE UNITE UNITE
UNITE UNITE UNITE UNITE UNITE UNITE UNITE
UNITE UNITE UNITE UNITE UNITE UNITE UNITE
UNITE UNITE UNITE UNITE UNITE UNITE UNITE

•   •   •

Paul and I have coffee at *Charlie's,* which has been open for a year but looks like an old college hangout. The walls are woodpanelled, covered with posters for films and art shows and photographs of old varsity teams in white sweaters and white trousers posed against a backdrop of painted elms. The wooden tables are bumpy with graffiti: phone numbers, names and dates, verbal and pictorial obscenities, "Frodo lives!," "Professor Braun reads Classics Comics." The day *Charlie's* opened they offered free coffee and donuts to people who would come in and carve up the tables.

It's crowded all the time now. A few days ago they put up a sign: "We want you to eat here, not live here." But the sign had no effect and this morning it's gone.

"Someone liberated the sign," Paul says.

He runs his finger along the rim of his coffee mug.

"Gratitude is no basis for a marriage," he says. "We don't have a word to say to each other."

I change the subject because I can't think of anything to say that won't offend him. Paul probably knows that he's spoiled and that being spoiled is part of his charm. (*Et moi?* I refuse to be charming—is that part of my charm?) I tell him that the National

Guard has taken over the schoolyard across from my apartment. There are jeeps and troop carriers parked on the basketball court and armed guards standing just inside the fence.

"Afraid the third graders will rise up and topple Tricky Dicky," he says.

He looks into his empty mug.

"A crisis should bring people together but it makes me want to grab whatever I can."

"Or whomever?"

"Bastard," he says, smiling.

When I offer to pay for the coffees he whips the check out from under the ashtray.

"*Nein, mon pauvre étudiant.* Loretta gets a real salary."

• • •

Benson comes out of the library as I'm going in. I hold the door for him and we nod. He's wearing black as usual, though it's a warm day: black shoes, black dress slacks, a black long-sleeved shirt. Pale, serious, black-clad, he looks like Hamlet, the kind of brooding, romantic Hamlet that Professor K. calls a serious misreading, an emasculation of the play.

Carla thinks Benson is the one who cleared the library's Milton shelf at the beginning of the course; no one's been able to find any of the books on the list Professor F. handed out.

•   •   •

"Proudhon?"

"No."

"Bakunin?"

"I've heard the name."

"Kropotkin?"

"I don't know. A Russian."

"A Russian, he says. Very good. Terrific. You're right, he is a Russian."

"If it's so important to know who they are why don't you educate me?"

"It's too late for you. You can't jump on the bandwagon now that it's rolling."

•   •   •

The walls enclosing the library courtyard are pseudo-gothic, yellow stone and narrow leaded windows with bits of stained glass in them, gifts from graduating classes. The fountain in the center is a square grayish basin embossed with leaves and grape clusters, with spouting dolphins at the corners. Cards affixed to each side, white with red letters, say:

POISON!
LEAD BASIN!
DO NOT DRINK!

Pilgrims of Mortality

Sitting on a bench reading *The Prelude* ("And, as I rose upon the stroke, my boat/Went heaving through the water like a swan"), I am suddenly afraid of snipers. I see the headline: GUNMAN SLAYS FOUR. I search the surrounding roofs. There's a fellow lying on the grass, an easy target, and some Japanese tourists taking pictures of each other in front of the fountain ("Actual Photo of Mr. Watanabe Taken Seconds Before his Untimely Death").

When the tourists leave I watch to see whether the door opens into the courtyard or into the building. Courtyard. I see myself zigzagging to the door, the rifle cracking above me, bullets punching holes in the fountain (poisonous water streams out) and whomping into the grass. Too late to help that poor bastard swimming in his own blood. I yank open the door and dive inside: safe.

· · ·

Cullen has been on the English faculty for two years but he likes to sit with the graduate students at *Charlie's*.

"After the Revolution," he says, "they'll make me teach Eldridge Cleaver."

"After the Revolution you won't teach anything, you'll dig ditches," Carla says.

"Why does everyone talk about ditchdigging? As if there's suddenly going to be this tremendous demand for ditches."

"For the bodies," Paul says.

Paul gets up to go to the library.

"How can you leave us?" Fran says, opening her arms and tilting her chin up, as if waiting for a kiss.

The rest of us suddenly turn into spectators and pretend there's nothing to watch.

Hand on heart, Paul quotes:

"The intellect of man is forced to choose perfection of the life or of the work."

He throws a kiss to Fran as he leaves. She sees Carla's frown and shrugs her shoulders.

"I know what I'm doing," she says.

"That's what I'm afraid of," Carla says.

Cullen says:

"I don't believe Yeats makes sufficient allowance for half-assed indecision."

· · ·

I try to work on an essay, a comparison of *The Prelude* and *A Portrait of the Artist as a Young Man:* "Stephen's epiphanies are more personal, more self-centered. In *The Prelude* Nature reveals *itself* and in doing so defines the poet. In *Portrait* ...."

I want something to happen outside so I'll have an excuse to get up. Anything: a fire, a car accident, an assault on the schoolyard across the street, a UFO setting down on Whitney Avenue.

• • •

The crazies stay up most of the night, then sleep anywhere. At nine AM Paul and I find three of them lying shirtless outside Professor F.'s office. On their backs, heads together at the base of a magnolia tree, they look pastoral and significant, like characters in a fairy tale. One stands and stretches. "Hi folks," he says to us, broadsmiling and rubbing the air with an open palm—his Eddie Cantor number. He springs up and chins himself on a tree limb, showering his hair and his sleeping friends with pink and white petals.

• • •

An undergraduate I don't know sits next to me in the dining hall. He's tanned all the way up his arms; his shirtsleeves are rolled to his shoulders. He shakes a cigarette out of a black pack, breaks it in two and puts the half I turn down behind his ear. He tells me he's just come back from Cuba: a shipload of them went for three weeks of work and fellowship. He describes driving to and from the fields in the backs of trucks, learning the Cubans' songs, sharing their food. Everyone's equal there, he tells me. There are no bosses, no special privileges. Everyone works with his hands, even Castro. Everyone builds houses, everyone farms. There's no theft, no jealousy, no unhealthy competition. Those evils are products of capitalist society.

I express doubts and talk about human nature, annoyed by his dogmatism but also dismayed to see myself in my father's role:

(MY FATHER: A dictator is a dictator.

ME: Batista was a dictator.

MY FATHER: Not a communist dictator. You young people think you can change human nature.)

"I was there! I saw it!" the undergraduate says. I think he has tears in his eyes.

"Do you know Spanish?"

"I learned some while I was there. You don't need Spanish to know what people are like."

We argue some more, then he stands, his eyes hurt and angry. He's got my number; after the Revolution I'll get what's coming me.

⋅   ⋅   ⋅

Another rally at the hockey rink. A black speaker says:

"If everyone here tonight will go out and off just one pig ..."

There are a few cheers and war whoops but more boos and a general grumble of disapproval. He is furious, curses the audience, breaks off and leaves the platform, a bodyguard of four men closing around him.

A young white man in a suit and tie gets up to speak. For maybe two minutes he says nothing but holds our attention, sweeping the stands with his eyes and leaning toward the microphone several times, as if just about to speak, then grinning mischievously and pulling away. Finally he does speak. Using the same passionate, heroic style we've been hearing all evening, he starts complaining about his father, how mean his father is, and something about warning him that this would happen.

A man approaches the platform and says, "This boy needs help."

The young man shouts, "No! You're the one who needs help!" but allows himself to be led away.

· · ·

Cullen, in the middle of a circle of undergraduates, says:

"The faculty understood the American racial situation long before the students knew there was one."

· · ·

When Carla is with Fran she looks small and tense. In general other women don't like Fran. Carla advises her not to get involved with Paul.

"There are other men around," she says, and then tells me it's all right to tell Paul what she said.

"You're happily married," Fran says. "You don't know what the world is like."

"You don't have to be single to suffer," Carla tells her. "You don't have to be black. You don't have to be poor."

Fran confesses that she sometimes needs half a bottle of scotch to get through the day.

"The couple who own the liquor store I go to told me I shouldn't drink so much. They *made* me have dinner with them last week. They told me to think of myself as their daughter."

Fran, it seems, is frequently befriended by grocers, landlords, shoemakers, waiters, and the people who own liquor stores, laundries, coffee shops.

"I don't believe you need much help getting through the day," Carla says.

"I've been trained to hide my feelings," Fran says, smiling.

Carla actually rolls her eyes; I thought that was just an expression.

They both look at me, as if expecting me to pick a winner.

• • •

Dinner at Paul's apartment is not pleasant. He and Loretta must have had a fight before I arrived because now they are not talking to each other. Loretta serves briskly, smiling at me, not looking at Paul.

Ignoring her, Paul talks energetically about the latest rumors: that there are paratroopers in the suburbs, that the Weathermen will storm the courthouse with stolen guns, that stores near the campus have had their insurance policies cancelled.

When Loretta talks to me Paul looks up at the ceiling, waiting for her to finish. She describes Professor Braun's attempts to seem absentminded, how he liked to wait until he's late for class or a meeting and then fling his papers together and run. She does a pretty good imitation, hunching forward and saying in a weary growl, "Loretta, Loretta! When am I going to learn not to get so wrapped up in my work?" Then she straightens up and laughs, surprised at having done it so well.

"How can you talk about trivialities at a time like this?" Paul says.

Loretta looks angry, then hurt.

When I leave, Paul insists on walking me downstairs. We walk back and forth in front of his building. The maple trees are just coming into leaf. From a distance the branches seem to be enveloped in green haze but close up the leaves are distinct, each a perfect miniature of a maple leaf, moist and translucent.

I tell Paul I'm sick of graduate school. If it weren't for the draft, I would quit.

"I don't want to be a scholar," I tell him. "I don't want to be a teacher. I just drifted into it."

"What do you want to be?"

"A doctor, a fireman, a lawyer, a truck driver, a shrink, a bricklayer, a chef."

"Well, flatten your feet. Chop off your big toe. Treat yourself to a tattoo: 'Victory to the V.C.,' across your belly."

"I've got to go," I tell him.

"I don' *want* to be like that," he says. "She brings out the worst in me."

We shake hands.

"Stone walls do not a prison make," he says.

He turns and walks to his door with a comic slouch: the inmate returning to his cell.

· · ·

There's a meeting in one of the dining halls. The University has offered free meals and a place to sleep to demonstrators who come for Mayday. A group of radical students argue that the oppressor cannot be allowed to disguise itself as a benefactor. Their principal spokesman, a fellow with a leather band across his forehead, says:

"Know your enemy. That's rule number one."

A student talks again and again about solidarity with the workers. After every three or four speakers he repeats his plea for a union of students and workers at the city's rifle factory. Throwing his arms out and down for emphasis, he looks like an umpire saying, "Safe!" after a close play at home.

The meeting goes on for a long time. Someone stands on a chair and shouts, "Enough talk! Talk won't free Bobby! Talk is shit!"

A young man wearing black-rimmed glasses reads from a prepared speech:

" ... volunteers whose names shall be drawn at random each day that the trial is allowed to continue, the selected individuals to sacrifice their lives on the courthouse step by a method of their choosing, one each day until this fascist oppression of our Panther brothers is halted."

At 2:30 AM the Dean nods toward the back of the room and says:

"We're keeping that good man from his home and family."

Everyone looks toward the door, where the college custodian leans against a wall, waiting to lock up. He waves like a sports star greeting his fans. We look and admire: here's a genuine worker, with paint-spattered shoes and gray overalls with wrenches and screwdrivers sticking out of the pockets. The meeting ends. People straighten tables, push in chairs and file out.

· · ·

Fran is a member of the Graduate Student Strike Committee and has been appointed student assistant to the Dean of Graduate Studies for the duration of the crisis. She carries a folder full of lists, schedules and phone numbers. People stop her on the street to ask questions which she answers clearly and forcefully.

The pay phone in *Charlie's* rings, the first time I've heard it. It's for Fran. She's excited, a warm blaze in her eyes. She drinks her coffee standing up, one hand on her hip. Looking down at Paul and me, she tells us about being propositioned by a truck driver:

"He said he'd give me fifty dollars to get in the back of his truck with him."

She laughs.

"I told him, 'Sorry, I don't have time.'"

· · ·

The National Guard have occupied the north side of Park Street. A single line of guardsmen is strung out across the fronts of apartment buildings, a Christian Science church, a gift shop, a photographer's studio. Overdressed in helmets, boots, guns, battle fatigues with pockets and pouches, they look ponderous, frightening but ridiculous, like deepsea divers out of water.

On the other side of the street a crowd of students and faculty members. We watch each other as warily as we watch them, afraid that someone may start something. Paul and I talk about how stupid it would be to be shot down on Park Street.

"What a blow to the future of literary criticism," he says.

But it feels like our responsibility to spend a certain amount of time across from the guardsmen.

Cullen crosses the street and goes up to one of them.

"I'm Doctor Cullen," he says. "Is there anything I can do?"

Eyes front, the guardsman says:

"Go home, Doc. What you can do is go home."

•　　　　•　　　　•

A phone call from my father.

"What's going on up there?"

"Meetings, a lot of talk. It's all right."

"Your mother and I think you should come home this weekend."

"No."

Ten seconds of dead air. Someone in the apartment below mine is clumping around. It sounds like a pegleg; maybe Long John Silver has moved in.

"Where do you stand on all this?"

"I'm sympathetic but sensible. Don't worry. I'll take care of myself."

Yes, well, I'm against poverty, discrimination, war and cruelty to animals. I'm for clean air, Chavez's grapepickers, Bobby Seale's freedom if he's innocent, bloodless annihilation of the grad school.

I go out. It's a mild evening. I can smell grass and warm soil. Two soldiers are in the schoolyard guarding their jeeps and trucks. Walking by them, heading for the quiet residential streets out near East Rock, I imagine what would happen if I ran at them, waving my arms and screaming.

. . .

The windows of the shops on Chapel Street, York Street and Broadway are being covered with sheets of raw plywood. All morning long hammers bang and there's a faint, sweet lumberyard smell in the air. *Charlie's,* boarded up, is dark inside, subterranean, a noisy cave.

I find a seat next to Kramer, who's in my modern fiction course. The only time I've heard his voice is when he read his paper in class: the usual cautious juggling of critical opinions of some book or other.

He glares at me. When I ask him what he's going to write his thesis on he explodes. Theses are shit, he tells me, books are shit, no book ever taught anyone anything, people who say they like to read are liars, books shouldn't exist while people are hungry and the jails are full of political prisoners. I ask him why he's in graduate school.

"I have my reasons."

"What are they?"

"You'll see. You'll be hearing about me."

. . .

There's a Mayday Eve party at the Handmans'. Mike is a lawyer. He wears mutton-chop whiskers and three-piece suits and enjoys using his deep voice. Carla is always poking him in the side and saying, "Stop trying to sound like Perry Mason," but he hardly seems to notice.

They are proud of their apartment, which they say is furnished in Contemporary Scavenger. In the livingroom are an old couch without cushions, a barber's chair, a yellow "school SLOW children" sign hung on the wall. The kitchen has a drugstore scale—your weight and fortune—and a traffic light sitting on a cabinet, flashing red and yellow. It seems very big indoors. Its size and drab metal color make it look like a weapon.

The tombstone in the bathroom is their prize possession. It's an old one, tablet-shaped and about two inches thick. The inscription is blurred, the stone covered with a patina of lichens, rust and dark green. A girl from the Milton seminar tells Mike, "You shouldn't have taken it."

"Yes, it was a crazy thing to do," he says. "I could have been disbarred if I was caught." He smiles at her.

The bedroom, where we pile our jackets and sweaters, is free of large *trouvailles* but there's a sign over the bed that says, "Sorry, We're closed. Please Call again."

Some of the girls make spaghetti. The steam billowing out of the noodle pot is red-yellow because of the traffic light. (Book I of *Paradise Lost?* Satan in hell: "a fiery Deluge, fed /With ever-burning Sulphur unconsum'd.") Fran scoops out noodles with a slotted spoon and dumps them on paper plates. She wipes the sweat off the back of her neck with a dishtowel. Hovering over her, Paul says:

"I didn't know you were so domestic."

There's spaghetti, wine, scotch, beer. People are determined to get drunk. They begin to act drunk as soon as they start drinking.

"Mayday! Mayday!" someone shouts.

The girl from the Milton seminar who told Mike he shouldn't have taken the tombstone tells me that the whole problem is that everyone wants a house of his own and his own backyard: suburbia is eating the country alive. In Germany, where she spent the summer, people live in neat little towns and go out to the country together on weekends, all in the same bus.

A girl I don't know is talking to Paul:

"I don't know you very well but I know Loretta and I just can't stand the idea of you not getting along."

Loretta sits on the cushionless couch next to Cullen, combing her long hair with her fingers. Cullen tells the "Go home Doc" story on himself and Loretta laughs and asks him what help he expected to give the National Guard. Was he planning to put the students to sleep reading excerpts from his thesis? Cullen looks dismayed; Loretta keeps laughing.

Some girl talks to me for a long time about peace.

"But it's not cement," she says. "None of it is cement enough." I nod, trying to catch on, and realize finally that she means "concrete."

Paul puts his arm around my shoulder.

"See? If you quit grad school you'll miss out on all this."

He waves his drink at the crowded room.

"Maybe I'll stay and be a fifth columnist like Kramer." (I've told him about Kramer's outburst in *Charlie's.)* "The enemy within."

Paul says:

"When we get to be department chairmen we can change the system." It's a grim joke we frequently share.

Carla tells me that she and Mike go diving in the Sound every Saturday even though they can't see anything but murk.

"After the Revolution we'll have to turn in our scuba gear."

She's had a lot to drink and her usual expression, a you-can't-put-one-over-on-me smirk has melted into a bland smile. She puts her hand on my arm.

"Where were you five years ago?" she says.

"I've often asked myself that very question," I say.

Paul and Fran disappear into the bedroom. Everyone knows, including Loretta, judging by the way she keeps chattering at Cullen. The party devotes itself to the single purpose of seeming to ignore what's going on. Fifteen minutes later, Paul comes back to the livingroom, drinking from a can of beer. Then Fran comes in with a plate of spaghetti. Nothing happens. I feel guilty about the fact that I'm disappointed. I find excuses for myself: human nature, etc.

"You're a bad boy," I tell Paul.

"*Carpe diem,* he says, and then: "You don't drink enough, you cautious bastard."

Benson arrives, even paler than usual and trembling with excitement. He reports clashes between students and guardsmen on Chapel Street and describes the teargas floating over the freshman campus. Someone else says he heard that a bomb has exploded at the hockey rink. Firecrackers or what sound like firecrackers go off outside.

Benson sits in the barber chair, his beercan on the chrome armrest, his head back as if he's waiting for a hot towel. Without irony he says:

"We're the custodians of the culture. We have a responsibility, like the monks of the Middle Ages."

Secret

I liked driving through this old, graceful neighborhood, the tall palms rising over the sidewalks, the Spanish villas set back from the road and half-hidden by flowering shrubs and cactus—full-size versions of the miniatures you see in pots on windowsills up north. Stretching out the trip from the airport to my mother's apartment was also part of the appeal, frankly, putting off, if only for ten or fifteen minutes, the demanding idleness of the visit. This time with the added challenge of her birthday.

The streets were almost deserted. A few cars rolled by, windows shut like mine against the July heat. One old woman shaded by a straw hat stood motionless while her poodle sniffed the shrubbery. A sprinkler waved a fan of water over someone's lawn.

I usually came down in fall or winter and only called on her birthday, but this was her eightieth.

Claudine hadn't come along. Well. It wasn't easy for her to get away from work, but the unsurprising truth was she had never gotten close to my mother. Claudine is not the kind of person who beats her head against the same brick wall forever. (She gave up on my annoying habits years ago, or so she's told me, though I'd say still makes an occasional effort to improve me.)

So only I would mark the occasion with my mother. She had no friends, only two or three people who looked in on her—mainly "the widows," as she called the women who had clubbed together to play cards and eat out after their husbands died off. Though my mother's two sisters had apartments of their own barely a mile away, the President was more likely to show up for her birthday than Rose or Florence, and he would have been more welcome, though she believed all politicians were liars and crooks.

I had invited my aunts—whom I'd never met; the family feud had been going on as long as I've been alive—for her seventy-fifth, the year after my father died. Neither attended the funeral. My mother condemned their callous absence as bitterly as she would have resented their ghoulish presence, but my father's death moved me to try to bring the sisters together. I sent Rose and Florence a few lines asking them to join us for coffee and cake. I phoned a week before the date. No answer, and no machines, of course. My mother doesn't have one either. "If it's so important, they'll call back," she says, though she lets the phone ring and ring. If it's so important, they'll bang on the door, I suppose, or send the police. Neither sister ever gave a sign of having received the invitation, and I never mentioned the attempt to my mother. Why buy trouble?

The villas gave way to pastel condos as I approached Ocean Boulevard. Right on Ocean, past motels and beachfront apartment buildings, here and there one spruced up but most a little shabby now, their white stucco stained with rust from balcony railings: my mother's neighborhood, showing its age. Between the buildings, I had glimpses of ocean and tourists roasting on the beach, getting the most out of their vacation. I pulled into an old strip mall not far from her apartment. It was mostly souvenir shops and beach gear now, but a few older businesses hung on at one end: the hardware store, a dingy grocery, a bakery staffed by what seemed to be the same old ladies in the same pink uniforms they wore when my parents arrived almost twenty years ago. Key lime pie and coconut pastries sat next to strudel and ruggalach, rye breads and layer cakes in the display cases. I bought a length of apple strudel, thinking that would more nearly please my mother than birthday cake.

"So you're here," she said at the door, and gave me her cheek to kiss.

"I stopped to buy strudel across the street," I said, handing her the small white box from the bakery. "Happy birthday."

"Now I'm an old lady."

"It's just a number."

"That's what you think."

"I think you'll live forever."

"Forever I don't want," she said, but pleasure at the thought tugged up the corners of her mouth.

In fact, she looked older. Her green eyes—her "famous" feature, her one acknowledged vanity—had lost some of the brightness that lasted so long, in spite of everything. Well, she was eighty.

She fussed in the kitchen, refusing my help, and carried a tray with two cups of weak coffee and plates with slices of strudel to the living room, her familiar forward-leaning walk, as if against a wind, only a little slowed.

I had never gotten used to my parents' Florida furniture: the pale carpet, the glass tables, the sand-colored chair and matching sofa, the wicker chairs and headboard in the "guest" room. But then I never understood their decision to move. They lived in Florida as if they had never left Brooklyn, shunning the beach, the golf courses, the pool, the botanical gardens and other tropical amusements. Even up north, my mother distrusted nature (which meant virtually everything outdoors) and nature here was even more foreign and unruly. My father hardly cared where he lived, as long as he had a book to read. For reasons unknown, perhaps even to them, they had let the tide of Jewish migration carry them along to this last stop. But they kept to themselves here too.

My mother unwrapped her gift, a semi-precious stone of deep mineral green, and put it on the table.

"Thank you."

"Claudine picked it out."

I reported briefly on Claudine's activities, on Emily's summer internship with a publishing company and Nicole's move to Providence with her boyfriend.

"That's what they do these days," she commented with mild disapproval but not much interest. These distant events had little reality for her. We ate our cake and sipped at the coffee. Her hand trembled as she brought the cup to her mouth.

"A regular party!" she said, mockingly.

"So how are the widows?" I asked, to make conversation.

"Busy! Always busy. Five of them went to … who knows where? Somewhere. A trip, a bus trip, of all things. A tour package!"

"Good for them," I said, though I knew my mother saw this as another proof of pathological sociability. "Did your friend Shirley go?"

"Yes, thank God."

Shirley was the widow who drove her to the supermarket once a week and "talked her ear off." My mother believed that listening to Shirley's chatter more than repaid Shirley's small service to her.

The afternoon unrolled in long stretches of silence, punctuated by my mother's complaints about one thing and another, including the shifting advice of the doctors who treated her mild Parkinson's: "It's bad enough they disagree with each other; you'd think they would agree with themselves, which they don't."

Later, I got up and drifted around the room, studying the bland prints of sea shells and beach grass. I slid the balcony door open and stepped out into the heat to look down at the bright oval of the pool for a minute or two.

"Some of your neighbors are swimming," I said when I came back in.

"Nothing better to do," she said. I don't think she'd been in the pool once since they'd moved in. Even when the girls were young and the four of us visited, she stayed in the apartment while we took our swim.

The glare from the balcony faded as storm clouds gathered. They let loose a brief downpour, the rumble and crack of thunder and rain driven against the glass, then sun again. The wet balcony steamed itself dry in ten minutes.

"Every day the same," my mother complained.

"That's a definition of paradise," I said.

She laughed, amusement briefly flickering in her eyes.

Of course, she didn't want me to take her out to dinner: the drive, the wait, the noise, the food no better than at home and ten times the cost.

"I flew down here to take you out," I said. "It's required."

"Do I have to enjoy myself?"

"That's optional."

"All right. We'll go, if it makes you so happy."

"Delirious."

I knew my mother would eventually turn to the subject of her sisters' long-ago treachery. Fifty years after the fact, it remained the defining event of her life, the unforgivable injury that filled and colored her days. She had made a kind of vocation out of that bitter memory. Ten or twelve years ago, when her sisters, one after the other, "followed her" to Florida—to this very city, to this part of the city—for the express purpose (she believed) of blighting her life here too, they added fuel to a fire that had never died down. In the car, watching the apartment buildings and clusters of shops glide by, she said, "Do I expect anything from the world? No. Do I ask anything? No."

Which was true in a way, but it would be equally true to say that she asked the world to be altogether different from what it was or what she perceived it to be.

"I learned to expect nothing," she went on. "Less than nothing. In my innocence, I trusted my own flesh and blood. On one fatal occasion. They taught *me* a lesson. I should thank them. Hah!"

"That was a long time ago," I said.

"Have they in all these years so much as tried to excuse themselves? Not that they could. Have I heard a word of apology? a regret? a shred of human feeling?"

"You been saying these things for fifty years ..."

"Who followed who to Florida? Answer me that."

"Do you ever run into them?"

"God forbid!"

All the time I was growing up, my mother's outrage hung in the air of our Brooklyn apartment. I tasted it in the scorched potatoes she put on the table, the leathery beef brisket, the cellophane crackle of fried eggs at breakfast. Even her dustcloth, smacked against the dining room chairs, seemed to express indignation at how Rose and Florence had treated her. To me, my aunts' treachery was simultaneously intense and vague. I knew that "those two snakes" would never cross our threshold again; that they should be barred from the synagogue, with no more religion in them than a stone or a stick (not that my mother went). I knew they had betrayed her, but never how. Their crime was literally unspeakable. When I was old enough (but still young enough) to ask directly, her green eyes blazed: "I wouldn't soil my lips to talk about it!" My father was no help. He shrugged and said, "Your mother's family," as if that explained it, which I suppose in a way it did.

For all of my mother's lifelong obsession with the terrible event, I never acquired more than a few scraps of real information about it. "The truth had come out" one evening at our apartment. The sisters didn't have the decency to be ashamed. My mother had physically pushed them out the door, turned the latch and never spoken to her sisters again from that day to this. A cousin—well-meaning, according to my mother, but with no idea of what she was dealing with—had attempted a reconciliation and failed. Rose and Florence had later become estranged from each other. Was the falling out over money? Sex? What else did people fight so fiercely about? I couldn't explain why the sisters would choose to move here, except to wonder if the same powerful forces that pushed them apart also drew them together. If Rose and Florence were anything like my mother, I could imagine *them* blaming her for anticipating and choosing out of spite the only place they could possibly live when Brooklyn became too much for them. Who knows? I don't even understand the simplest things, like how my mother heard they had moved. Maybe she sensed their malign presence.

When Claudine and I were dating, telling each other the stories of our lives, she couldn't believe how little I knew about my own family. Looking at my parents through her eyes, I understood for the first time how secretive they were. They would never tell me how they met. For a while I imagined they must be concealing some particular embarrassment or recklessness, but I think they refused to answer on principle or out of habit.

My mother surveyed the restaurant with a suspicious eye and glared at the fish fillet and vegetables on her plate. As she warmed to the perennial theme of how her sisters' falseness somehow proved that nobody was up to any good, she began absentmindedly spearing green beans and chunks of fish. Pretty soon she had polished off her food. So I would call the dinner a success.

Back at the apartment, I opened the Barchester novel I had brought along and lost myself in the lives of the Grantlys and Crawleys, laid bare by Trollope's unillusioned, forgiving voice. When I glanced up, my mother was looking at me.

"Still with the books!" she said.

"I'm afraid so."

"How many times did you read that one?"

"Only once before."

"I'm surprised."

"There are a lot of books in the world."

"Hah!" she said, offended.

My father's passion for reading would have been my parents' battleground if he had given her the satisfaction of fighting back. For as long as I could remember, he was settled in the living room with his current book before she had washed and dried the dinner dishes and clattered them back in the cabinets, only his hand moving as he turned over page after page. I felt that our love of books brought us together, though he paid no more attention to me than to her during those long quiet evenings, and seldom talked to me about what he read. The chores done, she sat in her accustomed chair, looking at nothing, and then more and more at him, at his absorption. Occasionally she tried to provoke him:

"Why do you waste your time with those books?"

When he allowed himself to be brought back from wherever his reading had taken him, he shrugged and said, "How else should I waste it?"

And yet they had been inseparable, a sturdy ecology of incompatibilities.

Now my mother and I replayed familiar roles. I read; she grumbled. It was almost comfortable, something we knew how to do together. At ten o'clock I said good night. In bed in the guest room, I read one more chapter and turned out the light. Letting my mind roam through the comfortably imaginary streets of Barchester, I fell asleep.

The next morning, I looked for chores to do. That had become part of the tradition of my visits after my father's death. He had never been particularly handy and neither was I, but the one-eyed man is king in the country of the blind, and the unskilled son is occasionally helpful in the elderly widow's apartment. Even changing a light bulb in a closet or clearing a drain was a feat. This time, there was the paper towel rack over the sink: one of the plastic arms had snapped off.

"I'll have to buy a new one."

"It can't be fixed?"

"Not by me."

She clicked her tongue.

"It's my treat."

"Get white, none of those colors that put your eye out."

"Don't worry."

I left the car where it was and walked, soothed by the blaze of heat and buoyed by a feeling that was like being let out of school or—forty years ago!—escaping the apartment to join my friends. The little strip mall where I had bought the strudel was a hundred yards away. I crossed the street and browsed along, in no hurry to get back, watching the tourist families and the few residents: a scattering of old women with plastic shopping bags, an elderly couple walking slowly side by side.

The old woman who caught and then riveted my attention held her bag not by the handles but bunched up in her fist. She was slighter than my mother, her face more angular, but there was no question that I was looking at one of my aunts for the first time. She had my mother's aggressive, head-first walk; she seemed to dare anyone to get in her way. Especially, conclusively, she had the same green eyes, as if my mother looked out of this woman's face—her sister's face.

"Aunt Florence?" I said, either drawing on an unconscious clue or guessing. It might have been Rose. She halted, still leaning forward. Her amazing eyes snapped up and locked on mine.

"It's David, Sylvia's son," I said, smiling.

The bluegreen flare of hatred that leapt from her eyes stopped me like a slap. We faced each other, a few feet apart, tourists dividing around us as if her electric hostility made a palpable barrier.

"No, no," I said, holding up my hands. "I'm so glad to meet you, finally!"

"You!" she accused, as if I had been lying in wait all these years. But I was determined to show that the feud had nothing to do with me; I held no grudge against her or anyone.

"I'd love to talk to you," I said. "Could we have a cup of coffee somewhere?"

"Stay away from me," she warned, her voice hoarse but strong.

"But Aunt Florence ... or is it Aunt Rose? I don't even know. It seems such a shame not knowing each other all these years."

Braving her angry stare, I took a step toward her. She raised her arm—the one holding the shopping bag, which had the name of the hardware store printed on it—the idea that it contained my paper towel rack flew through my mind—raised her arm, and pointed one long finger at me.

"A plague take you, and your family!"

"No, no, please. Why should we ..."

"A plague on your children!" she croaked wildly.

It should have been funny, this old woman in a housedress and running shoes near the fat orange rubber rafts leaning against the window of Tropical Dan's Surf Shop, tourists with Florida T-shirts and ice cream cones drifting by, the smell of coconut oil, the buzz of a small plane overhead, and this old woman, my long-lost aunt, arm outstretched like fate or the ghost of Christmas to come, cursing me and my family for no good reason. It should have been funny, but the naked power of her ill-will jabbed a needle of fear between my shoulder blades. I'm not superstitious, I knew her hatred couldn't really touch my children, but I wanted her to unsay those words.

"What can you have against me? Or them?" I asked, attempting a laugh. "Isn't it time, after all these years ...?

"Never!" she cried. A few heads turned, wondering why I was harassing this poor old lady.

"Why should you hate me?" I asked.

A dismissive wave—again my mother's gesture—and she moved by, keeping her distance, her eyes on me, as if I might try some mischief. Then on past the shops, vivid among the normal people, crackling with rage, until the curve of the sidewalk took her out of sight.

By the time I got back to the apartment, the sting of my aunt's hatred had turned into disgust at the whole ridiculous business—my mother's everlasting grievance and now this other old lady (and probably a third just the same) who would gladly see me and my family dead because of a fifty-year-old family argument.

"What is it?" my mother said, when she saw my face.

"Nothing."

I screwed the new towel rack in place and dropped the old one in the trash. I packed my bag and put it by the door. I sat across from her in the living room. Enough silence, I thought.

"I met your sister just now."

A look of angry alertness lit her eyes.

"Which one?"

"How should I know? She wasn't about to tell me. Smaller than you, same eyes. That's how I recognized her."

"Neither of them looks a bit like me. What did she want?"

"She wanted me to stay away from her."

"If she hadn't come down here ..."

"I know: she should have stayed in Brooklyn, but she's been here for a decade and today she was outside the hardware store, still furious, like you."

"What right does she have to be angry?"

"I have no idea. So tell me, finally: What happened all those years ago? What did they do that was so terrible?"

She looked at me.

"Why do you want to know?"

"I've been hearing about this terrible crime in our family for my whole life. I think I should know what it was about."

"Be glad it doesn't concern you."

"It does."

"It has nothing to do with you."

"She cursed my children. She wished a plague on my children."

"I'm not surprised," she said.

I was up now, standing over her.

"I am. I'm surprised that a woman I've never met in my life would wish harm on my daughters that *she's* never met, because you and she had a spat ..."

"That was no spat!" she said, outraged.

"So what was it?"

"If you think either one of them needs a reason to curse and abuse ..."

"*She* thinks she has a reason."

"I'm the one that has a right to curse, but I don't do it. That's the difference between us."

"So what terrible thing did they do all those years ago? Tell me."

"I don't like to think about it."

"You think about it all the time."

"I wouldn't give them the satisfaction," she said.

"Give *me* the satisfaction. Do I ask so much of you?"

She looked at me slyly, not answering the question.

"I would say, not so very much, over the years," I went on, "I'm asking this. Humor me."

"You don't want to know."

"I do. That's why I'm asking. The enemy is out there—if there is an enemy."

"If!"

"Tell me. I'm your son."

My face went hot as I said it. She sat straight in her chair, her green eyes glinting, her lips set.

"If you remember, after all these years," I taunted her.

"Remember? Don't I wish every day I could forget?"

"That's the last thing you want. This is the great event in your life; where would you be without it?"

"It destroyed my life!"

She didn't look destroyed. Something like a sly smile animated her lips as she looked up at me.

"Then tell me. Share the terrible secret."

She was silent a moment but not because she hadn't decided.

"Please."

"There's nothing you need to know," she said.

"I'm leaving in a while. Who knows when I'll be back?"

"What do you mean by that?"

She was right; it was a threat. Her stubbornness and my humiliation drove me to it, and a fleeting memory of my dead father's shrugging detachment. But she was more than a match for me. She was triumphant.

"Talk to me," I pleaded, "Tell me."

"Never!" she said, as my aunt had half an hour before. The sisters echoed and mimicked each other after fifty years of angry separation.

I saw clearly now what I suppose I had known for a long time, or should have: that secrecy, along with hatred, was the flame that burned in her, the heart of her heart. She regarded me smugly, gloating as if at some city slicker who thought he was so smart, imagining he could get something out of her. She enjoyed outwitting this stranger, her son. A shrewd peasant satisfaction lit her eyes, reviving all their old clarity and fire. Her skin turned rosy. She looked ten years younger.

Angry frustration flooded my chest, that old helplessness, but then something else, a kind of relief, a pleasurable sadness. The lightness of a desolation lifted my heart.

I had tried, I had done my best, but now it was settled. It was the end of something. I had lost the battle of wills, yes, but it was a liberating defeat. If she had told me, I might have had to love her.

Words without Songs

In memory of Ted May

The music sings in my mind. I've never been so prolific, though nothing comes of it. The best thing about this silent outpouring is that no one can find fault with it; even the fiercest critic (myself) is disarmed by the margin of vagueness that exists until notes are down on paper. ("Heard melodies are sweet, but those unheard are sweeter.")

The last time my hands made sounds at a keyboard—that last month—I wrote my three Dickinson songs. But I knew where my body was heading, if not how soon it would get there, so that small success was driven by an if-not-now-when-what-have-you-got-to-lose fervor and the shameful comfort of a ready-made excuse. (See what he accomplished despite his disability.) For three decades before that, the only piece I wrote was a four-minute set of variations for three snare drums—no pitches to fret over. It took me a year.

My composer's block dates to a few minutes after two PM on October 8th of my sophomore year in college, when I handed the manuscript of the opening movement (Allegro non troppo) of a Bartokian string quartet I was prepared to be modestly proud of to Professor Gruen. He glanced at the first page for a full four seconds, looked up (but not at me), and pronounced judgment: "One does not write like this any more." Gruen's Dodecaphonism, like other religious dogma, was an absolute belief based on no evidence, but that didn't make it any less devastating to my eighteen-year-old self. It would be misleading and grandiose, though, to blame him for damming up a flood of creativity (the budding composer nipped in the bud). More accurate to say he dried up a trickle that encouragement might have swelled to a shallow stream. Floods are not so easily turned aside. Would Beethoven have stopped composing if Haydn had told him, "One does not write like this?" I'm sure Haydn said that or something like it to his arrogant young pupil and Beethoven didn't give a damn or saw the criticism as a confirmation of his unique genius.

But Professor Gruen's verdict resonated with the doubts I brought to his office, and that (call it) unsympathetic vibration turned the continual murmur of insecurity I had sometimes ignored for an hour at a time into shouts of derision I couldn't. I stopped writing "my" music (that is, my imitations of Bartok, Barber, and Britten—the other "three B's," or "B-minuses," if you prefer), but the kind of music "one" did write in those years bored me. The result: one percussion piece in the decades between that afternoon and the Dickinson songs. ("I heard a fly buzz when I died" is the best. There's a moment of silence after the last sung phrase—"and then I could not see to see"—then the minor seconds come back, high and insistent, the jazzy fly outliving the expiring mezzo.)

The day after I finished them I started *Dorian*. An outline of scenes and musical numbers and a couple of pages of themes sounded out on the piano are the last things I wrote pen in hand. Then we left for a week—our traditional summer retreat, but this time my wife drove and the cottage we rented was "accessible." When we returned from what had once been a restorative vacation, I had lost ground and could no longer write: MS, yes; ms., no. (Even such feeble humor helps get us through the days here.)

Now, lying in bed in the morning waiting to be loaded into my chair or looking out the windows of the sunroom at cars entering and leaving the visitors' parking lot, I sing *Dorian* in my head.

Wilde's story is hothouse Victoriana, the paragraphs heavy with color and perfume: vermillion, emerald, gold, opal, azure, purple, damask, pearl, crimson, jasmine, musk, amber. What drew me to it in the first place (it has other resonance now) was the idea of a man eternally youthful while his portrait ages—not surprising given my own desire to stop time and—the same thing—escape the consequences of my actions and inactions. Also, I've never been able to resist a *bon mot* and Lord Henry, the author's evil twin, comes out with some of Wilde's best.

There are four-and-a-half characters in my opera: Basil Hallward, the painter of the portrait; Lord Henry Wotton, whose witty and corrosive cynicism sets Dorian on his ruinous path; Sibyl Vane, the young actress Dorian loves and then rejects; Dorian himself, of course; and—the "half" character—the portrait, which finds its voice as it loses its good looks.

Sybil's first aria is part of her performance as Juliet. It subtly recalls the music of Shakespeare's time (the balance of leaps and steps in the tonal melody, the minor third raised a half step to turn the final chord major) and a kind of artful simplicity. Her singing when she is with Dorian is almost monotone. Love renders her inarticulate or maybe I should say unmusical. Her final aria (her suicide notes?) combines the two.

I haven't solved the problem of how to set Lord Henry's witticisms. Clarity is important, the words have to be understood, but there should be an equivalent of the way these *bons mots* work, an unexpected musical twist. In the case of "*When one is in love, one begins by deceiving one's self, and one ends by deceiving others. That is what the world calls romance,*" for instance, maybe a simple melody that drops into recitative on the final few words?

The heart of the opera is a series of duets between the man and his portrait. The first begins as a solo: Dorian scrutinizes the painting, suspecting it has subtly changed, but rejects that notion as absurd until his portrait's voice confirms it by singing, its vocal line doubling the man's and then wandering away into nascent counterpoint.

Later, the portrait is hidden in the attic so that no one else will see the hideous physical evidence of the ever-youthful man's sins. Their difference in appearance is matched by a contrast in their vocal lines, but inversely, as far as beauty and ugliness go. Listen (I'm tempted to say, but you can't): A steady pulse of ambiguous chords in the strings as Dorian pulls back the curtain and regards his corrupted image. At rhythmically unexpected moments, the chords fracture into scalar runs (a flute in its dusky lower range) that do nothing to resolve the harmonic ambiguity. The man sings, sneering at the ruin his actions have created, his vocal line spiky and banal (a pseudo tone row that is my anti-homage to you, Professor Gruen). In response, the hideous portrait sings a flowing line (in Dorian mode, naturally) infused with compassion bred from the suffering it has taken on.

The lines cross and clash. At times, the portrait's notes seem to temper the harshness of the man's, but Dorian (the man) is enraged by this attempt at harmony and veers off in a new, uglier direction. He closes the curtain, shutting off the voice of his scape-self, and sings the last harsh phrases alone.

As of today, Sunday, October 3rd (the anniversary of the Gruening of my composing life comes up in less than a week), I have been at The Home for six weeks short of three years. It's one of the best facilities of its kind, with abundant windows for sunlight to pour through and rain to pour down, with (mostly) skilled and (mostly) compassionate staff (not you, Bertha) who understand that we residents are people not so different from themselves, with decent food, and the flexibility and facilities needed to help us live as fully as we can. A paradise for the paralyzed.

You don't want to live here.

Six years into the MS that ended my keyboard "career" (church organist, accompanist to a choir and a couple of soloists), then my teaching job, then, one after the other, basic skills I had mastered by the age of five, I had been on The Home's waiting list for just under seven months when I was interviewed by the professionally cheerful, improbably named Clara Barton (no relation to *the* Clara Barton, or so she claimed). I knew the toll my increasing helplessness was taking on my wife. I was the guilty source of her back problems, her exhaustion, the gradual wearing down of her optimistic spirit. Agreeing to an interview was the least I could do. People waited years to get in. I thought I could take the edge off my guilt by making my best effort and still not have to make that last move yet. Maybe we could hire help a few hours a day.

After a long, tragicomic history of disastrous interviews for jobs, a few of which I wanted (but that's another story), I effortlessly impressed Ms. Barton as a near-perfect candidate for The Home. It's a tribute to the quality of the institution that they moved me up in the queue because they thought I would be compatible with Steve, the chess-playing former chemist who is now my roommate. Like Groucho, I've never wanted to belong to any club that would have me as a member, but here I am. Possibly you can imagine the mixture of feelings I experienced seeing my wife revive like a parched garden after rain when she no longer had me to contend with.

For most of my life I've been a late bloomer, but I'm something of a prodigy when it comes to MS. The "progress" of the disease has been unusually rapid in my case. When I got here, I was among the most functional: wheelchair-bound, yes, but feeding myself easily with my one good hand, strong-voiced, able to cruise around at will in my power chair. At that time, calling the controller a "joystick" seemed ironic—moving and turning a wheelchair with a little rubberized knob not being what you would call a joyful experience. Now that irony is merely true. Regaining that easy freedom would be a joy. Not to mention the fact (that is, to mention it) that the vaguely nipple-shaped controller suggests another joy, also now inaccessible.

Three years less six weeks ago, Steve and I were roughly equal in our capabilities. He is still much the same while I have become one of those waited on hand, foot, mouth, etc. What we can no longer do, is done for us (in Bertha's case, to us). When I was a teenager, as insecure as most and more of an introvert, my fantasies often had me captive and bound, served and serviced by the prettiest girls in my class, who were unaccountably aroused by my helplessness.

Be careful what you wish for.

Now I am one of the "sip-and-puffers" who guide their power chairs, or try to, by blowing or sucking on a plastic tube: a hard puff to start, a soft one to stop; a soft sip for a left turn, a hard sip for right. It is every bit as tricky as you imagine. We are to blame for the traffic jams that sometimes block our wide, tiled halls—one of us stuck crosswise, or pointlessly circling, slowly banging into our compatriots in a kinder, gentler take on bumper cars. Sometimes these tangles bring a quiet, impotent hiss from one of the abler disabled, but rarely. You might expect that coming face to face or chair to chair with their own probable futures ("As I am now, so you shall be") would irritate people.

Generally it doesn't. Most of us learn the rudiments of compassion or can summon up a reasonable facsimile.

My devoted and thriving wife visits twice a week; we talk every evening, sharing news of the day (there's always something to report from this little world). We laugh, we say "I love you," we make kissing sounds. It's a long way from phone sex; call it phone cuddling. Our conspiracy of cheerfulness may not be the best choice, but I'm sure it's far from the worst. Then I am hoisted into bed like cargo, and she, at some point, goes to bed at that other home (lower case "h" but a more capital place to live), hugging what used to be my pillow (or possibly someone lying on my pillow—I have no way of knowing; if so, can I blame her?).

For years—BMS—I couldn't sleep on my back. Now that's what I do, having no choice. The boundary between necessary and merely desirable is flexible. At one time, the possibility of my wife's infidelity would have tormented me. Now—I can't say I take it in stride, obviously, but (wait for it) I do take it lying down.

So who am I if I can be both so much what I was and so different? Humans are shamefully adaptable. The self changes shape, shrinks or grows, depending on circumstances, and still insists it is one particular person.

For an hour or more a day, I dictate to my computer. I'm dictating this, of course. The voice recognition software has generally reconciled itself to my whispers. It still makes absurd errors, but occasionally mishears what I say in favor of what I would have said if I'd thought of it. (See above, for instance, where I said "quiet, impatient hiss" but it heard "quiet, impotent hiss.")

For another hour or two, I work on *Dorian*. And ask myself: Does an opera "composed" only in my mind exist? Or is the life of the mind, taken to extremes, no life at all? ("Occurrence at Owl Creek Bridge" and Borges' "Secret Miracle"—triumph of the imagination or solipsistic delusion?) See as well "Donovan's Brain," that staple of Million Dollar Movie and my blissfully squandered after-high-school hours: the mind, separated from the body and the world, turns insanely evil.

In case you're wondering, yes, I have considered the implied further question: when I become unable to express myself at all—no more dictation, no whispers, winks, or smiles—will I still exist in any way different from (not necessarily better than) a stone or a glass of water?

Now that MS is the biggest fact of my life, I'm less concerned than I once was about escaping the consequences of my (now more-and-more limited) actions, and Dorian's story has new meaning for me: the growing difference between the man and a portrait that rots like over-ripe fruit suggests my relationship with my failing body, if one can have a relationship with part of himself. (I've always dismissed Descartes' idea of the separation of body and mind—or soul, if you must—which I believe live and die as one. But MS tempts you to think otherwise. As the body responds less and less but the wheels of the mind keep turning, it's easy to imagine the "self" as a relatively healthy tenant of a condemned and slowly collapsing building. At the same time and on the other hand (that is, the self expanded, not shrunken), living every day in a wheeled contraption that is your only means of mobility eventually fools you into incorporating the chair into your concept of who you are.)

Back to *Dorian:* The idea of immortality through art is viciously parodied in the last chapter of Wilde's tale, the picture pristine and timeless, the man lying dead on the floor.

Which is what happens in my opera's final scene, the last of my Dorian duets. Dorian Gray (the man), selfish, corrupt, ultimately murderous, is finally overcome by something like remorse or disgust. His vocal line wars with itself, both seeking and undermining a tonal center. For a measure or two at a time, it blends with the liquid flow of the portrait's sorrowful compassion. The scalar runs of the earlier arias are subtly transformed, yearning now. Driven by his better self (multiple selves again!) or rejecting the implied kinship with his portrait, or both, Dorian (the man) takes a knife to Dorian (the painting). But the attempted portracide (no, computer, not "patricide") proves suicidal: the man lies stabbed to death, suddenly aged and rotten; the painting rejuvenates, becoming once again an image of perfect youthful beauty.

The duet becomes a solo (this time the picture sings alone). And here's the kicker, my *coup de théatre.* As the portrait regains its youth and beauty, its vocal line degenerates. The long, sinuous, melancholy lines give way to repeated rising three- and four-note phrases, a vulgar fanfare celebrating its restored youth and beauty.

In other words, wisdom and compassion are conditional and possibly temporary. Would my patience, my admirable perspective survive a miraculous return to health? Would my acceptance of the consoling embraces my wife may or may not be enjoying? Would I sit down at the piano and commit *Dorian* to paper, able to tolerate its inevitable flaws? I wish I could say yes. You hear about people transformed by illness or accident treasuring the lives they once took for granted. I'm a skeptic: how long do those transformations last? (See Chekhov's "The Wager.") If my mobility were restored, I would be fully alive to the joys of daily life for a while, certainly—for instance, the walk I used to take down Essex, left on Main to Awakenings, where they served my usual without asking, the bitter, foam-topped double espresso I lifted to my lips with my own right hand. The pleasure would be excruciating the first time, intense the fifth, but the hundredth? Would my enjoyment be compromised (as it was BMS) when I found someone else sitting at "my" table near the window?

I see myself as a kind of Dorian Gray, man and portrait, but with this twist: as my body degenerates, I become a "better" person, more patient and accepting, compelled to be virtuous by losing the power to be much of anything else. Of course I could choose to be "difficult"—a few of us are here—but that is not an attractive option when all the doors to accomplishment and admiration have been shut except this one: the power to face loss without complaint, to keep my spirits up, to entertain others with the dying embers of my wit and warmth.

So, when I have finished dictating the final paragraph of this reflection (How long has it taken to capture these few thousand words? I started at the end of September; it's late February now, one of those surprising warm days, judging by the fact, seen from my window, that nurses Nora and Beth are coatless on the bench near the main entrance, their faces tilted sunward. Five months, off and on. (Email and diary entries took some of my writing time, and there was the hospitalization after Thanksgiving (breathing problems (my weakening diaphragm, my fading voice—I have to position myself with my mouth against the microphone for my computer to hear me; it takes an absurdly "heroic" effort to make my chair go, turn, and stop.))))

When I finish this paragraph and the next (It's now Thursday, cold again, a few snowflakes. It took me all yesterday morning to climb out of the nest of parentheses I'd fallen into), I will roll to the day room if I still can and smile at the six or eight likely to be gathered there (almost certainly Benjamin, repeating a chapter of his well-known life story, and Alice, all eighty pounds of her, able to suggest positive energy without moving).

I'll whisper some little joke at my own expense that no one will catch. I will see and be seen. I will be what I never was or wanted to be earlier in my life—one of the group. I will play my small part as a member in good standing (sitting!) of this odd community, until my breathing stops (no more words) and I disappear.

On Hearing that an Old Girlfriend has Dementia

Of course the real losses and sadness belong to you and your family. Although we haven't been in touch for decades, I know there are sons and grandchildren (you and your husband—my rival then—married more than forty years). No doubt your family has had the usual rich history—a lifetime's accumulation of days and years. I can imagine your pain, forgetting, and theirs of being forgotten, having seen that happen to a few friends here. And what could be sadder than the unraveling of the fabric of a self that took so long to weave—all those memories, your knowledge and skill, your particular blend of kindness and wicked insight, your dark optimism (which I couldn't name at twenty but understood later, after you were gone).

So, no question: the loss and sadness are yours and theirs.

But I selfishly reserve a small piece of your misfortune for myself:

I choose to assume that (though maybe happy enough with your life) you have thought of our months together from time to time, as I have. In passing, let's say. Maybe, for no particular reasons, you've found yourself awake in the middle of the night remembering the all-or-nothing intensity of it, desire that reduced the world to shadows, lovemaking that knocked us out cold—how we would wake up after an hour or two, late for something. And everything else, meals together and walking from place to place, classes, the movies we saw, haloed by satisfied desire and desire reawakening.

It's pleased me to imagine that you've thought of those vivid moments too from time to time, maybe with affection—for your own youth if not so much for me. It's been a consoling part of my life to think of us still connected in memory across these thousands of miles and dozens of years. So the possibility of your forgetting me along with so many more important parts of your life I claim as my little corner of the general tragedy.

But it's sometimes in the nature of dementia to lose today and the recent past, leaving only a long-ago youth unerased, turning that distant then into now, not remembered but present. It could happen to you and someday possibly to me.

I can almost enjoy, hypothetically, what would in reality be the painful loss of my own fortunate life: my beloved and loving wife, two smart, funny daughters, the joy of watching grandsons learn the world, some work I'm proud of, travels, music, and all the rest. More than I deserve.

Still, I can imagine not knowing that I've lost those things while our brief romance comes to life again. Believing, for instance, that I still live in the top floor apartment of that rundown triple decker and it is, say, the night your evening class, which always runs late, goes on even longer than usual. It is well after eleven when you finally get here, standing on the sidewalk outside (your green raincoat keeping out the night's wet mist, the familiar red bag slung over your shoulder, your browngold hair).

On Hearing an Old Girlfriend has Dementia

I lick the flap of the envelope holding the front door key and watch it flutter down and land at your feet. Then lie back on the bed, waiting to hear your footsteps on the steep stairs.

Samson

I'm fine, fine. Thank you for asking. Holding my own. As the saying goes. No complaints to speak of. Nothing worth mentioning. No, I can't complain.

First time this year they've got a window open. First spring day. Nice breeze. The flowers that bloom in the spring. Tra la. Remember that one? Gilbert and Sullivan. *Mikado*. Have nothing to do with the case. It'll get cold again, I wouldn't be surprised. Nice for now. Spring breeze from somewhere. The South. Little flutter in the curtain there when the breeze blows, like someone's white dress when they're moving down the street.

Well.

Open one window and half of them claim they're chilled to the bone. Too hot yesterday, frozen today. Too hot, too cold, too dark, too bright, TV too loud, not loud enough. Enjoy fussing, if you ask me. Meat and drink to them. Make some noise, prove you're alive. Day or night there's no time you you're not hearing someone at it. A chorus of three or four, more often, moaning and groaning. There's worse things, I suppose. It's not my way, is all. Not my style.

It's the nurses you feel sorry for. What they put up with. Thankless task.

Also complaining about their children. *That's* a favorite topic. Expect 'em to be at their beck and call. As if grown children didn't have their own lives. As if there wasn't a world out there for them to enjoy. Never mind. If people want to complain, there's no stopping them. Life, liberty, and the pursuit of unhappiness. Hah!

I don't have much to tell you since the last time. No news is good news. Open a window, it's an event around here. Red letter day. A while back, a week or two back, we had something. Sound and fury that afternoon. One of 'em got away. Gladys. Escaped. Woman named Gladys, little stick of a thing, picked herself up and walked out the front door. They were short-handed, some of them sick, or other fish to fry. Not enough to go around. Security man asleep at the switch.

This Gladys made a break for it—absent without leave. Place in an uproar when they saw she was gone. They didn't tell you anything but you knew from the running up and down, doors banging. Came in here and looked under the bed! I said ... I told her, the nurse that's looking, "I haven't had a woman hiding under my bed for fifty years." Not that I did then either. They found her, still on the grounds, moving down the drive one slow step at a time: her getaway. Turned her around and back she came. "Where were you going, Gladys?" Nowhere, maybe. Away *from*. On the other hand, she's still talking about it: the ducks on the pond out there, cattails, daffodils. Sounds like a week in the country.

And all the time they're busy looking for Gladys, the rest of 'em are squawking "Nurse! Nurse!" Calls of nature not answered.

They're short-handed to begin with. Took more hours than you'd care to count to get this place half settled. Nice little girl looked in on me eventually, at long last. Squeaky wheel gets the grease. It wasn't Elaine. A new one. Elaine went somewhere else: greener pastures. A sweet little girl, though. Doing her best. They appreciate if you see their side, if you're not after them all the time, do this, do that, not complaining all the time.

I've still got my sight, still read. Glad of that. Clean clothes, a place to sleep. Know where my next meal's coming from. Food delivered, or they roll me to the dining room. Sometimes Mohammed goes to the mountain; sometimes the mountain comes here. It's not so bad. Count your blessings. One. Two. Try to think of a third one. Hah!

I read different things. I read the Bible some. Didn't used to. Not that I believe it now, not every word. Most I don't, but there's truth in those stories: food for thought. Great stories, some of them. Others I don't like. Abraham and Isaac? Asked to sacrifice his son? Hate that one. God says, "Go kill your son." Then changes his mind: just kidding, let him go. As if that makes it all right. Testing him. Blind obedience: keep your mouth shut and do what I say. Brutal kind of a God. Bully. Tower of Babel's the same thing—knock down someone else's blocks. Jealous.

You know the story of Samson? Now that's quite a story. Samson and Delilah. The Philistines. You know that one. I'll tell you something to make you laugh. Then I'll let you go. You know the story: Samson slaying Philistines by hundreds and thousands with the jawbone of an ass. Battles here and there. Delilah tricks him, learns his secret—he's strong if no one cuts his hair. She gives him a haircut when he's asleep and that's the end of all his great strength. Snip, snip, snip and he's just like anybody else. You know the story.

They capture him—and they blind him too. Still afraid of him. And tie him up, chain him. He's chained to the pillars of the Philistine's temple or whatever it is. So there he is, chained up and on display: thousands of Philistines in that temple mocking and celebrating. Their great enemy chained hand and foot, blind, weak as a kitten. Well, Samson asks God to grant him one last wish. He wants his strength back for just a single minute. That's his one and only last request. God doesn't say a word but the answer is "yes." Samson feels his strength coming back, pouring into him like sap rising in a tree, like a flood, like a flame of fire. He pulls on the chains that bind him to those pillars, pulls and pulls and brings them down, pulls them to pieces, and the whole Philistine temple comes down, crushing those thousands of Philistines, killing every one of them. One minute before they're jeering and dancing, the next they're smashed dead. Samson along with them, but he doesn't mind: out in a blaze of glory.

I read that particular story one or two times a week. Funny part is—I said I'd make you laugh—the funny part is I'm sitting here, reading that Samson story, and I imagine it's me in that temple. I imagine I'm Samson myself. Isn't that a humorous thing? Samson! Hah! Samson. It's true, though.

Because to tell you the truth, every once in a while I get tired of this situation. A little tired of it, a little impatient, at times more than a little. It happens. Tired and you might say angry—I admit that too. Yes, angry. From time to time. Not always, but so tired and angry sometimes I wish I was Samson chained to those pillars—yes—blind but strong again like I was, like he was and angry as him when he pulled those pillars down. In my mind I'm Samson—yes! hah! Samson!—bringing it all crashing down around me with the strength of my own two arms: all of this you see around you coming down, crashing, crushed to pieces once and for all! Everything! EVERYTHING!

Everything.

Mrs. Mintz's House for Sale

Her son-in-law carried her down.

At the top of the stairs he juggled her into a firmer grip. His damp breath bathed her cheek. Then down they went: jolting flat-footed plunges from step to step. She tried to see the stairs but found only the wall and, turning her head, part of the oak banister hanging in air.

"Don't drop me," she said, ashamed of the fear and supplication quivering in her voice.

"No chance of that," he puffed.

Her daughter Pearl directed from below.

"Careful, Arnie. Just three more."

Reaching the hall, he shuffled her quickly into the livingroom and dumped her on the sofa.

"Sorry, Rose. Are you all right?" he asked, panting. "You're an armful."

She groaned, though there was no pain, and waved him away. He flopped into a chair, for all his smart clothes and suntan not in good condition. And she was, as he'd said, a good-sized woman still. In spite of everything.

Her daughter refastened a button on the blue silk blouse and brushed her hair with quick strokes that pulled her head to one side. Then the lipstick. She had a horror of having lipstick put on by someone else, the wet waxy stick nudging her mouth like that. It was a violation. She tried to keep her lips shut tight but that annoyed Pearl, who began to prod.

Finally Pearl was done. Stepping back, she admired her handiwork with a painter's tilt of the head. Mrs. Mintz felt an angry sympathy for infants: stuffed into clothing, held over abysses, plopped down, propped up, cooed at.

"There. You look very nice," Pearl said.

"Fine," Arnold smiled from his chair. "If I were only ten years younger ..."

She pouted.

"All this fuss for that woman."

"It's not for her," Pearl said. "It's for you. You feel better when you're up and dressed decently. There's no need to look like a sick old woman."

But Mrs. Snow's call had set them going, spurred them into action. Pearl had run the vacuum cleaner over the rugs, dusted everywhere, making a clatter in the Venetian blinds and a quick clumsy glissando up and down the piano keys, carted newspapers to the trash, jabbed pillows into shape. And dressed *her* up to make her fit for Mrs. Snow's eyes. Arnold had left his shop to be here, to add his persuasive powers as a man of business.

Mrs. Mintz's House for Sale

"Mrs. Snow says she's received a very good offer," Pearl said.

"So that means the price I'm asking?"

Pearl shot a glance at her husband, meaning, here we go again.

"I don't know, Mom. All she said was a good offer."

"If it's less, it's not good."

"She didn't tell me how much. Let's wait until we know instead of arguing."

The weary voice of a mother stuck in the house all day with an unreasonable child.

The bell rang. Pearl went quickly to the door. Arnold stood up and twitched smooth the front of his red-and-black plaid jacket.

There were many many things she disliked about Mrs. Snow. Even her way of ringing the doorbell was offensive. When she pressed the button the chimes rang out too energetically and the cheerful tune they played sounded hypocritical. She didn't like Mrs. Snow's gray hair fixed just so, as if she had just stepped out of the beauty parlor. She didn't like her being so much at home here, sailing into the livingroom as if she owned it, not waiting for Pearl to lead her. Mrs. Snow had the knack of making you feel like a guest in your own home. For reasons no less real for being obscure, she detested the gray tweed suit Mrs. Snow wore today as well as all her other suits. Since meeting Mrs. Snow, she had come to believe that women in suits were not to be trusted.

Mrs. Snow made for the sofa, nodded to Arnold, sat, and pressed her hand.

"How are you feeling today, Mrs. Mintz?"

Disappointed that she hadn't said, "How are *we* feeling today?" Mrs. Mintz decided to believe that she had and responded, "*I'm* feeling all right."

"A lovely blouse," Mrs. Snow added, unfazed. "The color suits you."

She unzipped the leather portfolio on her lap. The amenities were over. Down to business. Mrs. Snow always had the air of being late for another appointment, making a conscious effort not to consult her watch.

"Well, I think I have good news for you," she said. "Do you remember that nice young couple with the baby who looked at the house last week? They liked it very much and they're making a good offer, a better one, frankly, than I expected you would get."

"How much?"

"Let me read the offer to purchase," said Mrs. Snow, slipping a single sheet out of her portfolio.

Mrs. Mintz remembered them. A tall lean boy with stringy hair, wearing work overalls, a fat baby lolling in a metal and cloth contraption on his back, and his little wife with a long mane of blond hair and a pudgy face—a baby herself. At first they were shy about coming into the bedroom but Mrs. Snow urged them on—"Mrs. Mintz says it's perfectly all right" (which she hadn't).

Mrs. Mintz's House for Sale

The girl peeked around the edge of the door and said, "We're *so* sorry to disturb you." But once well into the room she overcame her shyness: poked into closets and slid the windows up and down, letting in damp autumn gusts that ruffled the Kleenex on the nighttable and chilled Mrs. Mintz to the bone. She made her husband pace off the floor to see if their bed—how big could it be?—would fit in the room. Mrs. Mintz traced the rest of their inspection by sound: water gushing into the bathtub, tramping on the stairs, windows run up and down, the doors of the kitchen cabinets slammed, slammed, slammed, the downstairs toilet flushed.

Mrs. Snow got through the legal nonsense and read out the actual offer in dollars and cents. Warmed by righteous anger, Mrs. Mintz knew she had been afraid that it would be more.

"That's not the price I'm asking," she said mildly, pretending not to notice Pearl biting her lip. Mrs. Snow's smile didn't slip but Mrs. Mintz sensed the labor it cost her to keep it in place.

The three of them had at her.

Mrs. Snow reminder her than the offer was ten thousand more than the only other good offer they'd had in the months the house had been on the market. She explained again that many people didn't want the worry of caring for a big old house, especially one that, frankly, needed work, couldn't afford the heating bills, and the kitchen of course needed updating and was an awkward shape. It was a liability that reduced the value of the house.

165

"But this couple loved the house; the kitchen didn't bother them," Mrs. Mintz said, pleased with her shrewdness. Beating back the first wave of the attack.

Then it was Pearl's turn.

They both knew she couldn't live alone in the house any longer. If they had a trained companion it would be different but she insisted she didn't want a stranger in the house. She—Pearl—was at the house as much as possible but every time she left she had a heart attack thinking of her mother going alone to the bathroom or near the stairs. At the retirement home (they had put her on the list) everything was on one floor, there were handles to hold onto in the bathroom and trained attendants on call twenty-four hours a day, you only had to press a buzzer if you needed help. And good meals and people her own age to talk to if she wanted and not in the way if she didn't want.

Mrs. Mintz detected the tearful pleading underlying her daughter's sensible-sounding talk. She attributed it to the unspoken alternative that made Pearl feel guilty: that she should come live with them. Not that she wanted that either.

Pearl said, "I only want what's best for you."

Which was partly true, if at all.

"So I'll move," Mrs. Mintz said, throwing up her hands in apparent resignation and thinking that they had become a family of actors, Pearl and she herself too. "I'll move as soon as we can sell the house, not give it away."

Mrs. Mintz's House for Sale

Mrs. Snow said, "This offer is not giving it away. It's a great deal of money."

She didn't bother to answer. Arnold took over and Mrs. Snow retired to a spot near the mantle. Arnold sat, pulling up the knees of his red trousers. Pearl said the owner of a clothing store had to dress like that, to encourage business, but Mrs. Mintz didn't like the flashiness. He took her hand. They were all of them always taking her hand, like gypsy fortune tellers.

"Look, Rose. I understand how hard it must be to give up a house like this you've lived in for so many years. And it's a fine house, better than they build today. So I don't blame you for not wanting to move. But Pearl is right. You need the convenience of an apartment. A tough break but there it is. I can't tell you anything you don't know about the sadness of leaving here, but I can tell you about buying and selling, which is something I know a little bit about. Houses aren't sold like oranges in the supermarket where you pay the price they set, no questions asked. With houses there's an element of bargaining."

"Fine. Let them bargain themselves to the asking price. Every day I see in the paper that houses are going up."

"True. And a year from now you might get your price. But a year is a long time."

Pearl was pacing and even Mrs. Snow could hardly control her impatience and had to keep both hands on her portfolio. They were all in such a hurry, wanting to bundle her up and rush her out of her own house. The young couple were waiting (she felt as if they were at the door with their fat baby and their gigantic bed), wondering why she, an old woman who probably wouldn't live to spend the money, would make such a fuss over a few thousand dollars. Her daughter wanted to rush her into the retirement home. And from there she would be rushed into a nursing home. And then rushed to the cemetery.

When she pictured her funeral she saw the coffin bumped quickly in the rear door of an ambulance by attendants in uniforms, not a hearse. Lights twirling and blazing, sirens yelling, the ambulance speeds to the cemetery, flying through red lights, screaming around corners, bursting the iron gates at Montefiore in its rush to get her in ground. Quick, Mrs. Mintz, get underground, go away, make room for the living.

"I'll wait for a better offer," she said.

"Mother!" Pearl scolded, but controlled herself because Mrs. Snow was there.

Mrs. Snow sighed: "They're such a nice couple, and they like the house so much."

"They may be the nicest couple on God's earth but I'm not a charity to give people houses as a reward for their niceness. My husband worked hard to pay for this house. I can't throw his hard work away."

"Well," said Mrs. Snow, zipping her portfolio, "I'll tell them you don't accept their offer. There's a less expensive house they liked, but not as much as this."

"Tell them good luck and I hope they enjoy it."

Mrs. Mintz's House for Sale

She was proud of the firmness of her voice. There could be no doubt about her decision. Pearl walked to the door with Mrs. Snow. They whispered together in the vestibule for some time. Arnold returned to his chair and sat with his hands in his pockets.

"I think you're making a mistake, Rose," he said.

At least he had sense enough not to say more than that. He knew her mind was made up.

Pearl came back, smoldering. She went back and forth in front of the sofa, gesticulating like an oldtime actress making a tragic speech.

"I really thought you understood the situation, Mother. So what do you want me to do? I have a family at home that doesn't see me because I'm here with you and even when I'm with them I'm worrying about you, that you'll injure yourself. What about the bathroom? And the stairs? I can't run over here every time you have to pee. So what are you going to do, live up in your bed with a box of crackers to eat and a bedpan to pee in? And your heating coil to make coffee that only has to fall out of the cup once to set the house on fire?"

She dropped down on the sofa and looked to see if her words were having any effect.

"You know I don't want to talk to you this way," she said more gently. "I don't want to frighten you. But tell me what we're going to do now. It's an impossible situation. You know it is."

"I know, I know, I know," Mrs. Mintz wailed, spreading the fingers of one hand over her eyes and forehead in a gesture of grief.

Both her daughter's tirade and her sudden softening encouraged the welling up of pity for herself, for her undeserved misery. At the same time, she was unmistakably glad. Because the fact was that it was her house and they couldn't rush her out if she didn't wish to permit them. She'd slowed them down. It was her house and they were as helpless as babies until she chose to let them act.

She couldn't resist peeking through her spread fingers at the clear signs of Pearl's frustration.

From Ignorance to Bliss

"This is the story of my journey from ignorance to bliss," he said, looking from face to face—there were maybe twenty people in the Harrington Room, one of the church's smaller meeting rooms, about half newcomers; he'd seen some of them at services. He stared at his lap for a moment, collecting his thoughts or praying.

"It's not one of those stories—you've heard them—of a man who hits bottom and finds God in the wreckage of his life. Not in an obvious way. It's not a story of a man at the end of his rope, the frayed end slipping through his fingers, and God catches him. Those are important stories, but this isn't one of them. My story starts at a familiar place, where some of you may be at this very instant. I was more-or-less successful, as far as the world knew; comfortable enough, as far as the world knew. Am I describing you? You seem fine, as far as the world knows, maybe as far as your wife knows or your husband knows, as far as your children know, and maybe you think so, too: you're fine. Except ..."

He let the word hang and looked around the room again, from face to face, in no hurry.

"Except. Except for that nagging, hard-to-put-your-finger-on feeling that something is missing. If you're fine, why do you get annoyed so easily, or so easily discouraged? Why (not always, but more as time goes on) are you just the tiniest bit disappointed with that trip you looked forward to for so long, or that project at work, or that conversation with your spouse, or that new car, that TV, that meal in the restaurant people praised so highly, that glass of wine you bring to your lips? Why do you feel you're going through the motions? If the salt has lost its flavor, with what will it be salted?

"I moved to this town 28 years ago: arrived here with my graduate degree from MIT, my good new job, new house, beautiful and sympathetic wife—she still is; some of you know Ellen—, a healthy son, another child on the way. What more could I ask for? For a time, nothing. The excitement of those *good* things, the newness of them, carried me along for quite a while. Then the doubts crept in, the discouragement, the feeling that the world wasn't quite real, or I wasn't. A gap opened up between me and everything else, an emptiness ... no, I'm wrong: a barrier, as if an invisible something was clinging to me, covering my eyes, my ears, my mouth, my hands and fingers—I couldn't touch or taste or see as clearly as before—as directly—there was this little distance, this barrier, like a damp invisible cloth weighing me down. Outwardly, I looked the same, behaved the same; even Ellen who, as you may know, can spot a creature in distress at fifty paces, didn't know what I was feeling. I was that good at going through the motions. Maybe you are, too.

"Right now, some of you are thinking: clinical depression. He should have gone to a shrink. I did. Once I confessed to myself that I felt this weight, this disappointment—you can go on a long time before you admit it to yourself—and once I told my dear wife, I went to a therapist. Talked about feelings, childhood, anger, everything else people talk about. Took medication. My therapist was a good man, intelligent, sensible, practical, trustworthy, but none of his good work quite got at the problem. Medication didn't touch it.

"Nothing—not the therapy, not a loving wife and (by now) two children—touched the problem. I *was* at the end of my rope, though no one knew it except me and Ellen.

"That's when I discovered God. Biggest shock of my life. I'm an engineer. Cause and effect were my religion. Measurement was my prayer. I only believed what I could see with my own eyes.

"So did I see God? Not exactly, but yes, I did. And that's when I discovered the God-shaped hole in my heart. To be more exact, I discovered it *had* existed when it was filled, became aware of the wound when it healed. Here's what happened:

"It's an October morning. I'm in my office. To appreciate the irony of the situation, you need to know that my field is optics—specifically, at that point in my career, the shape of secondary mirrors designed to increase the resolution of compound telescopes. Blinded by the damp veil that had settled on me, I professed expertise in the physics of seeing, but even that knowledge seemed to be deserting me, the clean edges of formulae blurred by my misery and, if you want a more precise and scientific explanation, the intersection of my personal confusion with the sub-atomic scale at which certainty dissolves: the shifting quantum sands on which our solid universe is somehow amazingly built.

"I gave up and went outside. The lab sits in a few woodsy acres in these suburbs west of the city. The door nearest my office opens on a path through trees and shrubs and the stone walls you find everywhere in New England that used to mark the edge of someone's field. Through a light haze lit by sunshine, maple leaves were glowing, yellow on gold. It all may have looked the same when I arrived at work, but not to me because, the moment I pushed the door open, the veil lifted, dissolved, evaporated and I could see: not as before, but much better, much more.

"You probably know about the spectrum of what we call visible light, how it emerges, at its lowest energies, from the heat energy we call infra-red and disappears, at its highest, into ultra-violet and beyond that to x-rays and gamma rays. We have telescopes that can "see" those invisible forms of radiation. And I, as the door shut behind me, saw God's world for the first time, as if the spectrum of visible light my eye could perceive had expanded—not into those invisible bands of electromagnetic radiation but to a band of spiritual light whose existence I had never suspected. But there it was. I'm not talking about *a* vision. "It was *vision* pure and simple, a sudden and complete revelation of the presence of God in every molecule of existence. It was overwhelming and comforting, surprising and natural. It is what we were meant to see. I went home dazzled and joyful.

"Even in the midst of that revelation, my analytic mind asked if that apparent glory was a function of contrast, the return of normal perception after years of dimmed sight. I might wake up the next morning re-accustomed to the light, the wonder of it dissolved by habit.

"That was a decade ago. It hasn't happened yet.

"From the outside, my life probably looked much the same after that moment as it had before. Or the differences people noticed seemed small: I became a little more patient, a little more considerate and charitable; I'm usually in a better mood; I do more at church but not so much more. For me, though, everything changed. It felt like being in love. It *was* being in love—with the gift of the spirit. Now the spirit of God infuses every instant of my days and nights with meaning. It is as real as the taste of food, as real as sound and sight. The eyes of the soul see it, the soul's tongue tastes it, the soul's fingers touch it.

"That sensory awareness is what saves me: not for life everlasting, necessarily—I don't know anything about that one way or the other—but for life here and now, for life on earth. It's what I wish for all of you. That's why I've told you my story."

He scanned the room for a moment, looking from face to face before he sat down. The applause that inevitably followed seemed apologetic, as if people knew it was inferior to the silence that preceded it.

Fox

There was a fox in the yard. Sitting in a lawn chair in the shade of the birch tree, looking toward the little strip of woods that separated her property from the Weiners, Beryl saw it step delicately out of the trees onto the green lawn.

Foxes were rare here, or kept hidden, but it wasn't the first she had seen. The difference was this: It pranced halfway across the yard—brownish red, sharp black snout, thin except for its fat plume of a tail—then stopped, turned, sat, and looked at her, its black eyes staring—not in fear but in contemplation or connection, being to being, with a thrillingly familiar air of intelligent curiosity. The other foxes she had seen were shy above all else, they crossed open ground quickly. This one sat and looked, met her gaze, said, in effect, Here we are, you and I.

It was Paul.

At first, the shock of Paul's death had almost literally blinded her. His being gone was all she could see; the glare of loss blotted out everything else. Half the time she didn't know what was in front of her. Walking into the kitchen, she banged her shoulder against the door jamb; she tripped over the pile of newspapers that had grown in the living room.

After a time, though, her vision became abnormally acute or, to put it a different way, she lost the ability to see the whole of things, to see them in general. Tiny details caught and held her attention. She didn't see her yard or *that* tree but millions of leaves, branches, blades of grass, the ranges of tiny brown hills in the flower bed she would not plant this year. Each one of those minute details seemed to have its own meaning; they would speak to her if she could be patient enough to listen. Meaning was in the individual object, not in some idea of the whole. Before she saw the fox, she had been caught up in the overwhelmingly complex anatomy of one oak tree for she didn't know how long. The curvings and intersections of branches beyond what any artist could invent, the unique bays and peninsulas, the ragged coastlines of each of those tens of thousands of leaves—she felt that those infinite particulars explained what she needed to know, but also that it would take a lifetime to explore even a few of the tiny landscapes.

The fox rose and moved on but before he left the yard (back into the little strip of woods), he turned and looked at her once again.

No, she did not think that Paul had been reincarnated as a fox, that he spent his days and nights in the little wild spaces of these suburbs, learning to like whatever foxes ate, amused, as Paul had been by so many oddities, by his strange new existence. But she believed—she knew—that he had found a way to enter the fox for a moment so he could look at her and say, I'm still with you. Because it was not possible that he could have been annihilated by one small broken blood vessel—by faulty plumbing. Because love is stronger than death. Because, above all, she felt his presence: the little warm leap of her heart told her he was there.

She promised herself she wouldn't tell anyone. They would pity her, driven crazy by grief. They would thrust therapists on her, pills, consoling books: chicken soup for the grieving soul. No, it would be her secret and Paul's. They would be like two children who have a hideout they escaped to, and the greatest pleasure of being there was that no one else knew.

But.

Three days later, done clattering dishes back onto their shelves in the kitchen, her daughter Valerie took the stack of newspapers out to the recycling bin, then looked for something else to organize.

"You don't have to do all this ... improving," Beryl said.

"I'm glad to help," said Valerie, ignoring the undertone her mother had attached to the word that made it sound distasteful, no doubt resisting the temptation to lecture her about how unhealthy it was to let things go like this—to let herself go, to live in chaos that reflected and, she probably thought, fed her grief.

Valerie's lecturing posture (you might call it) was evident to Beryl and characteristic of how she saw her daughter now: firm, practical, relentlessly adult. What hurt Beryl most was not that Valerie had taken her father's death so much in stride but that it had strengthened and energized her. Yes, she might feel sad sometimes, she almost certainly missed her father, but she had blossomed (if that was the right word for becoming so steely). She was "moving on" with a vengeance.

Because she needed to defend herself and defend Paul against Valerie's acceptance of his death and because—admit it!—she could not not talk about the great, the miraculous event that warmed and thrilled her, she broke her vow of silence.

"I saw your father," she said.

Valerie stopped moving; held her breath, Beryl saw.

"He was ... I mean, he occupied the body of a fox that came into the yard."

A moment of appalled silence.

"Oh Mom," Valerie said. "Oh Mom."

As Beryl knew she would, but wasn't sorry she'd let the secret out, shared it, after a fashion. She met her daughter's stricken look with what she hoped was a calm and reasonable smile, wanting to reassure her, of course, but also facing the challenge, letting Valerie see that she would not back down, that she knew what she knew.

Last Words

There had been no question in Mary's mind about the decision to have Daniel at home and free of the technology that might keep his body going a little longer. If she knew anything, she knew that's what he wanted. And she wanted it; wanted him to herself. Although the visits from neighbors and Daniel's friends touched her and, yes, she needed the help of the nurse who came half a day every weekday; although she picked at the casseroles and loaves of bread people brought to the door, she was relieved (and even felt a tiny jolt of something like happiness) when everyone was gone.

"You shouldn't be alone," Mildred Colpitts scolded her.

"I'm not," she said. "I'm with my husband."

Mildred glared, her lips thinned by disapproving concern. She met Mildred's gaze and held it, until she turned away with a sigh and a shake of the head.

When Beryl Bainbridge rang the bell, she hid in the kitchen until she gave up, though Beryl would know someone had to be there with Daniel. But if she let her in, Beryl would turn the conversation to her own loss and grief, her one subject. They had nothing in common, not yet.

He was very thin, very weak. Turning his head or moving his hand had become a project. Yet he was so much himself. She couldn't say exactly what made that true, but whatever was fading away wasn't Daniel. His essential self was as present as it had ever been.

She slept on the sofa in the room that had become his bedroom, not only in case he needed her during the night, but to be near him. When it was late enough to be sure no one else would visit, she pushed the sofa across the floor, close to his bed. She welcomed the hard work of it, leaning her shoulder against the back, out of breath, her legs aching as it grudgingly scraped across the floor. That labor earned her the right to be close to him; it was a kind of journey to where he now lived. At the same time, there was something lighthearted about it, like girls at a sleepover pushing beds together. And, too, there was the memory of visits to her parents' house early in their marriage, so many years ago, carrying the night table that separated the twin beds in the spare bedroom to the far corner and mating the beds, the noise announcing to Mom and Dad: yes, we're going to make love, here, in your house—your daughter and this serious, humorous, energetic, talkative *man.*

In the morning she pushed it back so that people wouldn't think she had lost all perspective and decide they had to take sensible action.

She indulged in this fantasy: that suddenly the barrier his stroke had erected would fall away and he would speak to her one last time in the old way—the talk, talk, talk that had thrilled and exasperated her for so many years and that he loved so much—his voice returned to him at the last moment, like Samson in the Bible, who had his strength restored at the end.

More than anything he might say to her, she wanted to share his pleasure in saying it. Besides the longing, there was this seeming logic to the fantasy: that his failing body would become too weak to stand in his way and the words it had dammed up would pour out. But of course his body produced the words. When she imagined him speaking freely, the first thing he told her was that her reasoning didn't hold up, and he waved aside her argument that he *was* talking, which must prove something.

But in fact he said less and less.

It was gray February outside. For the last two days he had not made a sound, had not tried to speak. It was the deepest silence she had ever experienced. So when, this dank early morning, she saw his lips working to make words, she felt a thrill: maybe he was better. But she said, "It's all right. No need. No need."

She wanted him to know that the long romance of their conversation had continued these last two years, as far as she was concerned. Only the form had changed. And she wanted to spare him this suffering effort. Also, she knew that he would not let himself die until he had compelled his body to deliver one more message to her. As long as she could keep him from speaking he would not leave her.

She touched her finger lightly to his struggling lips. She met his eyes, which told her, Not likely, my dear; you won't shut me up now. She lifted the finger and took his hand, leaned closer as he fought a titanic battle to force his broken instrument to make sounds that would approximate his thoughts.

"Buh!" he said, squeezing her hand hard.

"Buh! Buh!" holding on for dear life, breaking her heart.

Then, knowing he had won, his body eased an instant before the words were out.

"Brave on," he said. And again, his still bright eyes fixed on hers: "Brave on."

Brave on: her marching orders, her burden and consolation from that moment on, the words he left her with.

His lips relaxed into something like a smile that lingered after he himself was gone.

Made in the USA
Charleston, SC
23 November 2015